Living and Loving in the
Shadow of The Valley

**Reflections on life and love, death
and grief, hope and rebirth.**

Thomas O. Burkig

E BOOK: 978-1-966131-34-2

PAPERBACK: 978-1-966131-35-9

HARDCOVER: 978-1-966131-36-6

Published by **Author Publications**: 2025

https://www.authorpublications.com

+1 (771) 203-5560

Dedication

This book is dedicated to Henry C. (Tata) and Gloria C. (Momo) Perez; husband and wife for 52 years, and the father and mother of my wife Gloria. They passed from this life nine months apart—their love was deep and forever. I also want to dedicate this work to our children, grandchildren, and Gloria's brothers and wives. Gloria's family became my family and is always in my heart. Finally, I would like to thank Pastor Mary Carbajal and Pastor Marian Deleon-Smith of the Mighty Wind Worship Center in Waco, Texas, for helping me to rise to my feet and begin my journey to hope and rebirth, following the death of my beloved wife of 53 years, Gloria.

Table of Contents

Introduction

Grief, as defined in the APA Dictionary of Psychology, 2007, is "the anguish experienced after significant loss, usually the death of a beloved person. Grief is often distinguished from bereavement and mourning…"

The book you are now holding in your hands and are preparing to read is an expression of my own highly traumatic experience with grief following the death of my wife, Gloria, in December of 2022. She and I had been deeply in love and married for fifty-three years. During our time together, we raised our daughters, cherished and adored our grandchildren, traveled across the world, and dedicated our lives to the people around us. When Gloria took her last breath and slipped away from the confines of this earth, I, too, found myself separating from my soul as I was cast into an emptiness devoid of meaning. I felt myself withdrawing and dying in the lack of her presence. I began a long journey, moving from the depths of darkness toward a light that I longed for but thought I might never reach. I am still traveling along that road, making slow but now steady progress. I can feel myself beginning to breathe again—coming alive.

What you are about to read is a story of how Gloria and I joined together and what we experienced as we grew in our love for one another. I cannot tell you Gloria's story—only my own. And so, I will reflect on my own life before, during, and after my time with her. I will share with you my understanding of what death is and what it means for myself and the world around me. You will learn that I was an adopted child, and throughout the course of my life, I was exposed repeatedly to instances of death and sorrow. As a young man (prior to my knowledge of the fact that Gloria even existed), I served in the United States Army and spent three tours of duty in Vietnam. And yet, despite my familiarity with death, I was totally unprepared for the loss of the woman who had become the center and meaning of my life.

This story is part of my effort to heal from my loss and grief. As I write I am remembering, pondering, and deeply grieving. Gloria died of liver cancer, and I will take you through our years of life as that disease slowly ravaged her body. I will teach you, ultimately, that grief is in our lives to assist us in returning from our own deaths due to the sorrows of losing what we love most. You will grow to know me at a level I have rarely shared with others. There will be points where you will laugh, cry, and wonder whether or not I am even sane. All I ask is that you stay the course with me as I wander in my despair from one thought to another. If you are presently grieving or seeking knowledge of grief in general, this work will help you on your own journey. We are all moving toward that moment when we will no longer walk this earth. I loved Gloria with all my heart and still do, and now I want to share with you our life together.

Chapter One

Choice

"He knew he was driving straight into the center of his pain, the vortex of the Great Sadness that had diminished his sense of being alive."

Wm Paul Young…The Shack

In the movie Good Will Hunting, Robin Williams, playing the character of a therapist, is talking with Matt Damon, a client, about issues of loss. Williams states to Damon, "You don't know about real loss because that only occurs when you love something more than you love yourself." A profound statement, which I have "doctored" up to some degree, for the purpose of helping you to understand the book you now have in your hands. My version of the above quote goes as follows: "You don't know about real grief because that only occurs when you lose something, or someone you love, more than you love yourself."

I have lost Gloria, my wife of fifty-three years, whom I loved, and still love, more than I love myself. I am enveloped in grief.

***

In my experience, as I continue to struggle with Gloria's death, there are two major components to the grief response: the first is what is usually referred to as Anticipatory Grief (before a loss occurs), and the second is Grief due to Actual Loss. Anticipatory Grief, in many situations, may never be experienced simply because loss or death may occur in unexpected moments: unforeseen accidents, acts of nature, etc. The word anticipatory implies that one has time to prepare.

Death, as we all understand, can occur without warning, and subsequently, due to its unforeseen presence, no preparation is possible. When death just happens, grief due to actual loss follows immediately and can be absolutely terrifying. It manifests in your mind and body without any control on the part of its victim. It is deeply intense, both mentally and physically, even to the point of crippling you, stopping you "dead" in your tracks. And, in its most extreme form, it can cause your death.

Grief, anticipatory or actual, in either form, is a devastating emotional response to any of the countless memories associated with whatever or whomever you will lose or have lost. It comes in many forms: anger, sadness, depression, anxiety, crying, withdrawal, all unwanted expressions of hopelessness and despair. It can be triggered by situations or thoughts you are unaware of.

And it can present itself unexpectedly, without regard to where or what you might be doing. When grief presents itself, there can also be a very clear, very disturbing "knowing" on the part of the griever that he or she has died or is dead but is still continuing to move and breathe.

My own grief has generally expressed itself in the form of deep sadness, repeated episodes of intense crying (for the most part in private), anxiety (often not visible to others), and periods of withdrawal. It has now been almost two years since Gloria's passing, and I have realized that I have become less intense in my "overt" grief responses, but crying and/or withdrawal continue to cling to my being and can still trigger bouts of mild anxiety. I still believe, at times, that it will never end.

Anticipatory Grief involves emotional responses that arise in relationship to an expected loss and in "planning" for that loss: financial arrangements, funeral arrangements, getting your house in order, etc. For Gloria and I, thinking ahead to her death was a very disturbing undertaking, but, at the same time, we were still thinking: she was still active and alive. On the other hand, grief due to actual loss simply arises—no planning can be engaged in. It becomes a natural part of what must take place after the loss occurs. Emotionally, however, grief is grief regardless of whether it is anticipatory or in the moment. This book will introduce you to the joys and the sorrows of the life my wife, Gloria, and I shared with one another and the world we lived in for over 53 years. This is a book about love, death, grief, and rebirth.

***

The date was April 16, 2022, and Gloria and I were sitting in a small office in the Interventional Radiation Department (IRD) of Scott and White Hospital in Temple, Texas. After almost nine months, we were once again

5

preparing ourselves for yet another embolization procedure to slow the growth of cancerous lesions eating into her liver. She had, since January of 2019, gone through one Microwave Ablation and four Embolization procedures. Our doctor was reviewing with us the fact that the cancerous growth process had been slowed due to her regularly scheduled procedures. Still, he pointed out there was an increase in the size of one particular lesion on the surface of her liver that was becoming of concern. We knew, and had known, that the possibility of rapid growth of older lesions or development of new lesions was always a possibility. We also understood that lesions would be present on the surface of her liver, which might be responsive to treatment by medical intervention, while lesions within the liver would not be treatable, except at great risk to her liver's ability to carry out its function. The embolization procedures had been difficult for Gloria, and it generally took her body almost a month to fully recuperate from each intervention. We also understood that recuperation did not equate to healing. We were prolonging life, not saving it. Regardless of whether the procedure went well or not, new lesions would continue to surface on and in her liver.

Our Interventional Radiology Specialist sat with us and informed us of what we might be facing. The bottom line was that Gloria had reached a point in her treatment where continuing the embolization procedures could be dangerous and might shorten the amount of time she had left. He explained that if she were to undergo another procedure, she might be subject to a fifty percent chance of going immediately into liver failure, which could result in her death. The choice for her was to understand that either with or without the procedures, she had come to the point where death could no longer be appeased. She had reached a point where no specific time frame could be offered: it was just a matter of time—as it always had been.

We were in shock. We sat, holding each other's hands, as both of us began a silent flow of tears. The doctor also, was silently tearing as he relayed this information to us. He talked to Gloria about her bravery in facing her gradual development of liver cancer. He told her that she had stood straight and bravely faced the procedures she had undergone, and she had done so with a determination to live that he had rarely seen in other patients he had worked with. He told us how he wished it could be otherwise, but such would not be the case.

She was, at that moment, as she always had been, in the hands of God. Despite the praise and encouragement in his words, neither of us felt even remotely brave as we sat there processing what he was saying. And as he completed his summation of what she was facing, he also indicated to us that he, himself, had the beginnings of NASH.

***

Gloria died, and for some mysterious reason, I lived. It didn't seem right. My daughters were with me, but each of us was lost in our own sorrow and grief. We were going through the motions, trying to focus and be responsible. We managed to struggle through the first few days following her passing, discussing what would need to be done (putting what we had discussed in anticipation into action). It seemed that there were at least a thousand issues we had to address and take care of: she would be cremated, a Celebration of Life had to be planned and scheduled, a host of friends and relatives had to be notified, and her personal property would have to be distributed in accordance with her wishes. I needed (it was essential) to keep myself busy, and I decided my first focus of attention would be on what to do with her clothes and jewelry.

In the months preceding her death, she and I had talked at length about who would receive specific items of jewelry, and I had prodded her into making a written list of who would receive what so there would be no arguments or disagreements.

Several days after her death, my daughters and granddaughters and I gathered in the bedroom that Gloria and I had slept in for almost four decades, and, following her written instructions, pieces of jewelry were given to each person. We spread rings, necklaces, crosses, earrings, and random pieces of personal gems (all representing years of memories of our life together) on our king-sized bed. I sat quietly watching, occasionally providing brief histories of certain pieces as each person received or chose what would be theirs. Once all the listed items were distributed, we began a search of drawers and jewelry boxes, revealing what seemed to be an endless number of clasps, pins, and random pieces of costume trinkets and pendants. All was laid out for consideration. At times, I felt a sense of detachment as I wondered what it was that we were doing or why we were doing it at all. It was Gloria's most personal property being handed out, with both our lives being held within each piece being given. At times, we laughed, and at other times, we cried as I shared story after story about particular items and how they came to be in her possession.

Once all the jewelry had been divided up, we moved on to her clothing. Clothing was easier and less personal because most of it would not really fit any given family member who wanted or received it. There were hats, jackets, sweaters, various shoes, boots, and scarves, all of which were carefully considered and then quickly whisked away. Whatever clothing items remained were then folded or stuffed into plastic bags and later taken to Goodwill and other organizations for distribution. I wanted to move through the process as quickly as possible because I recognized that the longer I waited, the less inclined I would be to give her belongings away.

A final consideration on that day that I needed to address was Gloria's painting utensils and supplies: brushes, palettes, tubes of coloring, various pencils and charcoals, and a multitude of sketchbooks, and art books discussing the world of drawing and brushwork and how to carry it out. Relinquishing those items was a slow process, and not everything went. Still, it was a beginning, a beginning with no clear ending, and it seemed as though my entire life history was disappearing before my very eyes.

I can now say, without any hesitation, that our home, despite the dispersion of Gloria's personal property, will always be filled with love and memories (neither of which can ever be given away). There is always something here that serves as a reminder of her presence. She has remained with me at all times. I could give her "things" away, but my thoughts are not subject to such passage. Now, sitting alone in the silence of my home, I wonder what has happened to my life. She is gone, yet she is always with me. My purpose, the meaning of my existence, has been ripped away.

***

During Gloria's last two years with us, she became increasingly interested in issues of the spirit and the role of God in her life. She read continuously, from different spiritual orientations, about what the end of life would be like for her. At a certain point, when her energy levels were slowly dwindling, and her ability to concentrate was becoming more difficult, I took on the role of reading daily to her. She was fascinated with stories about how different people have passed from this life to the next. We also explored in depth, the work of Death Doulas (although she never requested to be ministered by one). I would find a story to capture her imagination each night, and off we would go. There were times when I wondered if she was able to follow along with what I was reading to her, but she always seemed alert and willing to listen, and she always asked for more. I knew she was seeking comfort in the journey that lay before her. She was strong in her spirituality, and she loved her God. Later in this book, I will return to this subject.

***

As I close this chapter, I would like to take a brief

moment to address my feelings and how they are and have affected my writing as I talk about my life, my marriage, and my seemingly never-ending grief since she was taken by the cancer that spread throughout her liver.

My experience of grieving has been frightening to an extent that I have never come in contact with before. I need to note here that I was a mental health professional, and I had devoted my life to assisting others in overcoming their own frustrations and inabilities to meet their life needs. I was good at what I did, although I wonder, at times, about exactly what it was that I did that was so effective. I have, to this point in my life, been unable to help myself in the manner in which I had helped others. I have read _C. S. Lewis's A Grief Observed_ and have thought deeply about his surprise in finding that his grief, in the loss of his wife, was so enmeshed with fear.

I, too, have experienced, disturbingly, outright fear. I have been scared without understanding why. I have been avoiding that issue because it seems to reflect a weakness, a failure on my part. I am addressing the issue of fear on a daily basis, and this book is a representation of my struggle to come to grips with my fear of living. In the next few pages, I intend to explain how Gloria and I first met and what our life was like as we grew in love. In doing so, I will move forward and backward through my own life and my experiences growing to adulthood and how they impacted who I am today. I fully intend to share my deepest, most disturbing, most embarrassing feelings revolving around my panic and anxiety following Gloria's diagnosis and eventual death. It may seem that I digress at times (which I do), and

I may repeat myself or go off on tangents that might seem vague or irrelevant. I sincerely hope that what I have to offer you, as you ponder it, will serve to inspire and motivate you as you engage in your own search for healing from the pain of loss and grief.

Chapter Two
When Words are Not Enough

How do I love thee: let me count the ways...

I love thee with the breath, smiles, tears, of all my life;

and if God choose, I shall but love thee better after

death.

Elizabeth Barrett Browning

(Sonnet 43-1850)

It's true: I didn't know what to say. How do you let someone know that you love them, other than just telling them? I said it to her all the time, but now it doesn't seem (at least to me) that it was enough. How could I tell her that I felt helpless to make things right other than to just say it? I kept thinking I was missing something which, once recognized, might change the direction we were moving in. A terrible feeling of pain continues to this day (although less frequently) to rip through my mind, crushing me under its weight. I don't want to feel the sadness and sorrow that has become a constant in my daily existence. And, more importantly, I didn't want her to feel it either while she was still with us. She was, and always will be, the love of my life. She is my heart, and deep inside, I know she struggled with the same feelings. I was her heart, too. Our love surpassed any verbal expression either of us could ever offer. We simply were.

Gloria knew that I was not right. We were both in shock. We were trying to be strong for one another, but I was feeling a weakness that could and would bring me to my knees if I allowed it. We both cried, sometimes unexpectedly, for no known reason. I was strong and weak at the very same time, if that makes any sense. She was well aware of the fact that at some point after her death, I intended to write a book about our life and our love. She knew that I would try to put into words the world that we created for ourselves and how, in bringing those words to life, they would come to me at a profound cost.

We had, over a period of several years (ten to be exact), been going through anticipatory grief. Our physical and emotional reactions to the process of her dying were slowly entering our consciousness. One might think, erroneously, that because we had time to process the actual act of her death, it might be easier to deal with it when it finally happened. Nothing could be further from the truth. There is no such thing as preparing for death, even though we might mistakenly delude ourselves into thinking it might be possible.

Plans can and should be made if there is time for doing so, but those plans do not prevent grief. The cold, hard fact is that Gloria physically suffered and died from liver cancer, and a part of me went with her. For a decade, we were both dying at the very same time. I was not physically wounded, but a part of me was actually slipping away, unable to hinder its advance. Anticipatory grief, at best, gave me a few moments of deep breathing before actual, soul-crushing grief descended into my being like a heavy dark cloud. Oddly, I was able to recognize that the pain of grief was actually a healing process that I would, whether I agreed to it or not, have to go through. And I knew that for me, there would be no such thing as "redirecting my thoughts and behavior." I would not simply get a grip on my despair. When she was finally gone, I found well-meaning sentiments like, "She's gone to a better place, now," to be useless defense mechanisms spoken by well-wishers trying to protect themselves against their own feelings.

Grief, for those who experience it, is a harrowing journey down a long road leading toward an unknown, unwanted, distant future. And it cannot be avoided.

***

I pace back and forth for what seem to be endless periods of time, fighting off moments of anxiety. Then, with a sense of determination, I sit before my computer, writing and rewriting these words. Even months after her death, it seems impossible at times for me to focus on what to say or how to say it. What exactly can I, or should I, put to paper? I can't hold her in my arms and make everything go away. I don't possess a magic wand that I can wave and somehow turn time back to before it all started.

I wonder, "When did it start? Was it ten years ago, twenty years?" I will never know. I do know that she was exhausted. I could look into her eyes and see that. I also know that at times, she was afraid, although she was trying not to show it (probably trying to protect me). Her eyes told me everything. But, as for me, I was not afraid; instead, I was stricken. I was stricken with a grief so deep and dark that I found it almost impossible to think or talk about it. And yet, neither could be avoided. We had to talk about it back then, and I have to talk about it now. My sadness, my sense of emptiness, overwhelms my thoughts, and at times, I wonder whether I can take another step. I can be standing or sitting and be stuck firmly in place, unable to move. And yet, I keep going. I didn't want to think about losing her, but I knew such thoughts couldn't be restrained. I wanted to take her place, but such an arrangement did not seem to be a part of the "grand scheme." I have difficulty defining what part of me died with her, but somehow, I know it was my heart (my soul). I feel a void where she once was (and still is) and I know I will not be able to replace it: it is gone now forever. The emptiness itself is like floating in nothingness: no color, overwhelming silence, loneliness pushing down on me.

At times, over the years, I would fantasize about trying to bargain with a higher power that I would go first, and she would follow much later and meet me (where? I was never quite sure). I remember so many times, as we turned off the lights for sleep, she would laugh and say, "Hey, wait for me." Then she would lean over and give me a goodnight kiss. Now I wonder where it was that I was going, that she wanted to come with me? I, in turn, said in my mind, "No. You need to wait for me. We take our trips together, so don't you leave me behind while you journey on to places I can't go."

I understand as I write these words that I will never be able to adequately convey to the reader what I am really feeling. At the deepest levels of my sadness, there are no words. At times, I might come close, but I will never do more than scratch the surface. And so, with such knowledge in mind, I will try to introduce you, the reader, to the story of our love, knowing full well that each one of us has a story of our own to tell, as well. Every story is different: some sad, some happy, some inspiring, some cautionary, but a story is always there in all our lives, waiting to be told.

***

In my mind, I suspect that I am skimming across the surface of a vast body of water, not unlike a water strider flitting from here to there without stopping: to stop is to drown. I have only a vague idea of what I want to convey to you, and I'm not sure what is most important as to what is the least. Our life together and our expectations were oftentimes fleeting and unpredictable despite our endless attempts to make them seem rational. Without occasional meandering and outright craziness our relationship and marriage would not have been what it was. Gloria and I, like everyone we have ever known, joined together, both of us naïve and knowing at the same time. Through the years, our love shaped the many experiences and wonders we shared and served to create the life we sought to build. It was, and still is, a very good life (although difficult at times for me to see).

***

It was mid-morning and Gloria was stretched out on the living room couch watching the never-ending stream of Christmas movies, which endlessly occupy the television screen beginning just after Thanksgiving and ending just after the entrance of the New Year. Christmas had passed by five days, but the "holiday" movies continued on, one after the other, as if knowingly waiting for the close of the old year. I was sitting close by her, reading a book and glancing at the TV screen occasionally. I would light-heartedly harass her about her liking of those always predictable renditions of holiday cheer being played out with different sets of actresses and actors. The same story over and over. She would find my remarks humorous, smile and laugh at me, and then ignore me as I continued to question her about what was so attractive in all the repetition: my way of assuring myself that she was alright. I would inquire her about whether or not she thought that the actors in the shows really did all the Christmas tree decorating in the plush settings being presented.

To my sadness, as the days after Christmas passed by slowly, leading to the New Year, I began noticing a deeper tiredness beginning to settle into her face, and I could see a "far off" gaze reflected in her eyes. In Vietnam we called it the thousand-yard stare. When the look became observable to others, we knew that those experiencing it were not in the present time. They were not with the rest of us; instead, they had gone to another place in their minds, perhaps a better place or a place of silent memories. Gloria had slowly developed that look.

On the day before New Year's Eve, while resting on

the living room couch watching her shows, she told me she needed to go to the bathroom. And because walking was becoming increasingly difficult for her, I would help her to stand up, position myself behind her, wrap my arms around her, and we would slowly walk to the master bedroom bathroom. She was so soft and vulnerable, and it felt so good to hold her close to me. As we approached the bathroom, I suddenly realized that she was sinking slowly downward onto the carpeted bedroom floor. I was unable to prevent her from going down; she simply collapsed and rolled onto her back.

I tried to put her back on her feet, but she was unable to help me, and I couldn't lift her by myself. She had no strength, no muscles to rely on, but thankfully, she was not in pain. I laid a pillow beneath her head and covered her with a light blanket, explaining to her that our oldest daughter, Celeste, who was already on her way for a visit, would be arriving momentarily and that we would get her back up on her feet. She was not in distress and just smiled at me with that distant look still in her eyes, and told me that she was okay. A few minutes later, Celeste arrived. We quickly assessed the situation and attempted to bring her upright but could not do so. She was completely lacking any needed strength to assist us. At that point, we decided to call hospice, explain the situation to them, and ask for assistance. They readily agreed to send someone to help us and encouraged us to stay with her until they arrived.

Celeste and I sat on the floor with her talking and making sure she was as comfortable as possible. She didn't complain, worry, or show any signs of physical difficulty.

Within fifteen to twenty minutes, a young woman arrived at our house, introduced herself as a hospice care Social Worker, and said she would help us get her standing again. Three people turned out to be the solution, and within a minute or so, we had her back on her feet and I was able to support her final steps to the bathroom. She wanted me to stay with her but asked me to close the bathroom door because she didn't want other people watching her using the toilet. As I closed the door, the Social Worker offered to assist her. Gloria looked at me, rolled her eyes, and told me that she didn't want anyone's help but mine and the Social Worker could go ahead and leave. Her comment surprised me and irritated me (I don't want to admit this), both at the same time. Here she was, in my mind, being stubborn and resistant (maybe even vain). I turned to her and scolded her that I could not help her by myself, nor could Celeste, nor anyone else do so by themselves. All the while, Celeste and the Social Worker are standing by the other side of the door, listening. I explained to her that hospice was there to assist us, and she needed to be respectful of that. And, while I related those thoughts to her, I felt like total shit for doing so. I was afraid. Deep down in my soul, I knew that she was nearing her time for this life to end. I could stand there, break down, and cry or get upset. I chose (without thinking) to be upset. I wasn't ready to let her go. The Social Worker (of course) was not offended by Gloria's remarks and wished us an uneventful rest of the day and a Happy New Year, and quietly went back to her Holiday.

Once Gloria had finished using the toilet and cleaning herself, she allowed Celeste to come in with us, and together, we assisted her in walking back to the living room to the couch. As I started to flush the toilet, I glanced into the bowl, and there was a splash of bright red blood in the water and more in her stool. I could feel my heart slowly sinking inside me, and I knew that she would not be with us much longer.

When she was once again lying comfortably, I sat next to her, took her hand in mine, tears in my eyes, and told her I was sorry for becoming upset with her. She looked at me, squeezed my hand, and said, "Not to worry, no big deal." Her attention then returned to whatever Christmas movie was on the screen in front of her.

***

Later that afternoon, we noticed that her legs appeared swollen, and her skin had taken on the texture of soft clay. When we pressed our fingers against her flesh, a deep pit would appear and stay there for a long period of time. Her liver was failing, and what we were observing was what doctors call Pitting Edema.

Chapter Three
The Beginning of the End

Going on a little farther, He fell on his face, praying,

"My Father, if possible, let this cup pass from me!

Yet…not what I want, but what You want!"

New Testament: Luke 22:42

In May of 2013, Gloria and I invited her brothers and their wives to visit the famous "Flea Markets," held each spring in Canton, Texas. Canton Trade Days is spread out over four hundred and fifty acres and offers every kind of used, new, or outdated merchandise you can possibly imagine. Thousands of people from all over the United States (and other countries as well), aware of the limited time frames in which the Market would open and close, would make short or long trips to Canton. It was a unique experience to be able to say they explored row after row, and mile after mile, of booths, stalls, and buildings, offering whatever could be displayed for consideration and purchase.

Gloria and I had decided to travel there in our newly purchased RV and stay in a park located close to the festivities. Her older brother and his wife and son would share our house on wheels with us, while her younger brother and his wife would stay in the same park with their own RV. Early in the morning, we loaded up our luggage, got comfortable in our vehicles, and set out in a tiny caravan heading to Canton and arriving at the RV park around noontime. Everyone was excited about getting our homes on wheels set up so we could begin exploring what the Market had to offer.

Our first order of business before going shopping was to get physically situated in our assigned spaces and hook up to water and electricity. It had become Gloria's and my routine that as I was backing our RV into an assigned space, Gloria would walk behind and to the left side of the vehicles, guiding me in with hand signals. In addition to her direct assistance, I would reference each of my rearview mirrors to ensure I was backing in straight and on target. As we began our usual routine, I glanced to my right rearview mirror, checking my position, and then I looked back to the left mirror for her directions. But instead of seeing her guiding hand, what I saw was Gloria lying on the ground, not moving. At that very same moment, I became aware of her younger brother sprinting at full speed toward where she had fallen. I slammed my truck into park, cut the engine, and leapt out the door, running to her as fast as my legs would carry me.

Her brother reached her first and was holding onto her arms as she struggled to right herself and get to her feet. As I arrived at her side, I could hear her crying, and I saw blood coming from a nasty gash on her right forehead/eyebrow area, flowing down across her right eye and cheek. She was holding her right wrist, which was quickly swelling to the size of a jumbo egg shape. Both her hands were pulled up tightly against her middle chest area, and she was complaining of pain there. I immediately reached out to her eyebrow and pinched the wounded, opened area together with my thumb and forefinger to stop the flow of blood.

And, while at the same time I was talking with her, trying to calm her, I became aware of the fact that I was beginning to tremble. I had a mild sense of the jitters sweeping through my body, and I sensed that I was on the verge of falling into a state of panic. Tears were welling up in my eyes. I managed, with great difficulty, to keep my focus on her, though, and got her, with the help of the others, to a spot where she was able to sit down.

As she regained her composure, she explained to us that she had tripped on a rock, which she had not noticed as she was backing me in. As she fell, she landed chest-first on a hard PVC sprinkler tube that was sticking up from the ground. The tube snapped when she fell on it, and she landed on the right side of her face and her right hand and wrist. I quickly checked her chest and after assuring both myself and her that no further injuries were evident, I finished moving the RV into position, unhooked the truck, and off we went to the Athens Hospital Emergency Room, some thirty miles down the road. We were both shaken, but she was alert and calm, and I was slowly allowing myself to regain my composure.

In the ER, X-rays and tests showed that she had a severely sprained wrist, a bruised chest, and a nasty cut above her right eye. The cut required glue rather than stitches due to its location. A chest X-ray revealed a mild case of bronchitis (which she was not aware of), and she was provided medicine to treat it with. The ER doctor explained to her that she would be very sore for several days, but otherwise, she would be okay, and her wrist would gradually lose the swelling and return to normal. So, she got patched up, discharged from care, and back to Canton we went. Gloria, wearing a sling for her injured arm, an ace bandage wrapping her swollen wrist, and touting a shaven, superglued right eyebrow, was tired but otherwise back in business. She was slightly dazed and yet still trying to be upbeat about her situation. She indicated to us that she would rest for the remainder of that day, as much as possible, and we would then rent a motorized scooter for the duration of our stay.

I, in direct opposition to Gloria's positivity, on the other hand, had been shaken to my core. Never in all the years that we had been married had I ever seen her physically hurt in the manner in which this freak, unexpected accident presented itself. I found myself trembling and near tears on several occasions, despite knowing she was going to be alright. This was a new and disturbing experience for me, and I tried to keep my emotional reaction from her or the other family members. I'm not sure my efforts were effective. Thankfully, after a short rest, Gloria rose to her situation and began journeying through the marketplace on her scooter, searching for a "good buy." We all kept a close watch on her, but she seemed to be taking everything in stride and was having a good time.

The rest of our trip was uneventful and we made it

back home without further incident. After unpacking and settling back in, we scheduled a follow-up visit with our primary physician to ensure her injuries were on the way to healing. The findings revealed in his follow-up, however, were destined to change our lives forever.

Our Primary Physician, after reviewing the medical records related to her injury and bronchitis, referred her for further testing (possibly to ensure that the PVC pipe had not done more damage to her chest area than was originally thought). The tests he ordered included a sonogram, and it was through that procedure that it was discovered that her spleen was enlarged. She had an ascites (fluid) build-up in her peritoneal cavity (the space between her abdomen and her abdominal organs). Those findings were clearly not related to her injuries in Canton. Further testing then revealed the presence of liver disease: her liver had become cirrhotic and was swollen, not due to her fall but rather to something unidentified that had been taking place in her body over a long period of time, something which had not been previously detected.

Later, after interviewing with another specialist, we were informed that there was no treatment for cirrhosis of the liver and, eventually, her liver would succumb to the spread of cancer. Over time, her liver would begin to fail, and death would follow. Her situation was considered terminal. I can now say that, in spite of the devastating news she had been given, she was also told that she was only in the beginning stages of liver dysfunction and she still had several years of life to live; her disease would progress slowly. We did not learn that immediately, however. That knowledge came later through visits with a renowned Liver Cancer researcher to whom she had been referred. At the time of the initial diagnosis, we were both in shock, stunned by the information we had received. Gloria was given a diagnosis of NASH (Non-Alcoholic Steato- Hepatitis).

Within two months of Gloria's diagnosis, I had my first experience with what is known as Anticipatory Grief: I had a massive panic attack (which I will discuss in detail later in this book). As my panic attack resolved, I began to realize, at some vague level, that I had been taking our life together for granted.

Over the years of our marriage, I simply lost sight of the fact that sickness and death would eventually make their presence known to us, just as it does for all sentient beings. Our life, in both of our eyes, had been picture-perfect. Certainly, we had undergone the usual medical concerns most families must face, and we had the usual struggles with our children's behavior and health as they moved toward independence. But Gloria's diagnosis of NASH was beyond anything we had ever imagined possible in our future. We just assumed that we would age gracefully and pass away peacefully, hopefully together, lying asleep in bed one night—the end of a beautiful story. Truly, life had been good to us, and we had been good to ourselves in our care and love for one another, as well.

And just maybe, in the process of living our lives somewhere along the line, I think we had unconsciously assumed that a higher power was rewarding us for our commitment and devotion. We were not wrong in thinking as we did.

The only thing we forgot was that all life, regardless of how it presents itself, can be dangerous and unpredictable. Life and death are two sides of the same coin: one cannot be present without the other.

There were many lessons to be learned following Gloria being hurt in Canton and then being diagnosed with a terminal illness. Importantly, we slowly began to understand that her condition (our condition) was neither a reward nor a punishment. Certainly, we both turned inward to find our God, seeking an answer to the question of WHY. I, in my search, found a degree of solace in the New Testament. In the book of Matthew, 5:45-47 (KJV), it states that "ye may be the children of your Father which is in heaven: for he maketh his sun to rise on the evil and on the good, and sendeth rain on the just and on the unjust." These words spoke to me and reminded me that that simple truth was ongoing and ever-present in both our lives ever since the day of each of our births. I remembered and spoke to the fact that every day and every night, our lives had been a living miracle. And I remembered and spoke to the fact that we are all children of both joy and sorrow.

As the years following her diagnosis went by, I admit that I experienced times when those words in Matthew were hard to accept, but I did not forget or reject them. And I now know that it was because of our trip to Canton that I suddenly woke to a new reality, forcing me to begin looking at life through a totally different lens, one without any guarantees.

Before Gloria's diagnosis, I considered myself to be an agnostic at best. I believe that each of us, as human beings, is responsible for the life we choose to live (I was right in such thinking). As I grew to adulthood, I experienced a great deal of confusion within myself as to how to relate to any organized religious approach, considering what I had been exposed to in my childhood, my adolescence, and my life as an adult serving in Vietnam. But the one thing that always sustained me was my relationship with Jesus Christ. And, as time flowed through Gloria's and my life, I found Jesus living within me, and I within Him. I did not verbally share this awakening with others, though: Gloria was my only confidant. Following Gloria's death, I sought out grief counseling, and it was there that I began to put my own belief system into words.

I will say, at this time, that I do not believe that if I pray hard enough, be honest in all things, and live a loving life, a "God" will reward me with some desired outcome. Instead, I believe that being honest and loving is an outcome I seek, and praying for that life is not necessary. What is necessary is that if I want something or need something, I will work hard to achieve or acquire it, and it will come to me only if it comes to me.

I do not live my life because of some religious teaching insisting that God rewards those who imagine they are righteous and correct about what He wants or expects. I have lived my life in the manner in which I have because it is right to do so, and I want to live in that way—not because

I have to—but rather because I want to. My God, simply put, is the God of Life and Death. I rejoice in the presence of life, and I suffer and grieve in the presence of death. I was shocked and then awakened when Gloria was injured in Canton. I did not lose my faith. Instead, it was strengthened, and it has evolved.

Now, as I continue on my personal journey through the Valley of the Shadow, I realize that I have somehow survived a broken biological family, a broken adoptive family childhood and adolescence, three tours of duty in a war zone, the near loss of my first daughter, and untold other events, all reflecting both rain and sunshine. I believe in the message of Jesus Christ, and whether I like a given outcome or not, I remain strong in that belief and continue to move forward in whatever life is yet for me to live. I do not like or want the hurtful, negative, traumatic events that come with living. I am not expected to like them, only to know they will come. Good and Bad, for me, are (like life and death) two sides of the same coin.

Gloria was a positive, active, loving person, and as time moved forward, we began to process her diagnosis of terminal illness mentally. And in spite of her advancing sickness, her attitude remained positive, and she continued to interact fully with the life that surrounded her daily. Together, we faced the growing issue of how we would approach her final years. We grew to know the reality of anticipatory grief, but we did not succumb to it. We faced the fear that was presented to us and learned to continue living.

Most importantly, we kept moving. In many ways, I have concluded that she was, at least outwardly, much stronger than I. We visited with friends and family and traveled freely throughout the United States as her disease slowly progressed. We made plans, not for her inevitable death, but rather for what we would do while she still lived. We cried and held each other. We laughed, and we continued to live. That is what life and death are really all about.

I will share more of my thoughts about the role of my God in my personal life and how my God has sustained me (sometimes against my will) as I have moved through episodes of pain and overwhelming sadness following Gloria's death. Grief is unique to every individual experiencing it, and your knowledge and understanding can lead you in new directions if you will allow it to happen. I truly believe that rebirth after loss is possible. I am working on it, but it is not yet done.

***

Gloria, for reasons unknown to me, was resistant to surprises: surprise birthday parties, surprise family events, and surprise trips. She wasn't obsessive in her resistance, but she did like to plan things ahead of time. I, on the other hand, was open to spontaneous, unexpected experiences, providing, of course, that they were pleasant in nature.

One of Gloria's ongoing interests revolved around various activities related to what I call sewing. I am totally ignorant of issues of embroidery, knitting, sewing, quilting, and whatever else might be included along those lines.

However, I will add here that I was able to learn, with the use of a "rack (?)," how to knit or crochet (whatever it's called) winter scarves. I would make them during the cold weather months when going outdoors was difficult, and football was dominating the TV screen. I actually got very good at it, and I made scarves for all members of our family most of our friends, and I even gave them out to veterans and to people in general. I just handed them to whoever wanted one. Most members of my family seemed amazed that I could do "something like that." It was definitely something different for me, and I really enjoyed it. Oh well, moving on.

Gloria was totally engrossed in matters of creativity with cloth, thread, and yarn (and she painted, as well). Over a period of several years, she attended different classes to improve her skills (which, to me, were already very impressive). She had what she called a beautiful sewing machine, drawers full of threads, cloth, needles, hooks, rulers, and a shelf full of books. The list goes on and on. She learned to make table runners, worked with yarn, made clothing items, and even started to crochet (?) a king-sized warming blanket for me.

That blanket was the first and only thing she had ever set out to make specifically for me, and she started working on it just prior to the time when her cancer began aggressively attacking her liver. She never finished it, and following her death, I folded it up and placed it in a basket in our bedroom closet. I could not let it go. My sister later finished it for me and it now lies at the foot of my bed.

The one thing Gloria hadn't done was to make a

quilt, which is (at least in my eyes) a daunting task in itself. She always expressed an interest in doing so but, for some reason, never followed up with it. As fate would have it, though, I somehow became aware of a quilting festival scheduled to take place in the State of Virginia (I have no memory of how that information came to me). I kept the knowledge of that event to myself and decided that I would surprise her with a trip to an unknown place for an unknown purpose.

I talked with my daughter Heather, who works for a major airline, about my plans, and she said she would assist me in securing plane tickets and departing/returning information. Once it was determined that a trip was doable, I sat with Gloria one evening and told her that I had scheduled a mini-vacation and made reservations at a nice hotel in a certain state at a particular time. I explained that the trip was a present from me to her, the reason being: BECAUSE.

As I expected, while seeming to be somewhat intrigued, she reminded me that she didn't like surprises. She bugged and badgered me, but I remained closed-mouthed and uninfluenced by her efforts to pry the information from my locked jaws. She resorted to attempts to manipulate our daughters and granddaughters (whom I fully informed of my plans) by bribing them with money or goods, but they just laughed and turned to other matters. Time went by, and two days before the trip was to take place, I finally spilled the beans. She was actually ecstatic (which I expected she would be), got excited, and wanted to go shopping for a few new items of clothing to take along on the trip.

Our journey to the quilting festival was a huge success, and I surprised myself by enjoying it more than I thought I would. We found ourselves wandering through row after row of demonstrations, booths, and quilts of every color and thematic depiction that could be imagined. The craftsmanship on display was amazing. Gloria took every opportunity to stop and talk to vendors and attendees, who willingly shared their knowledge of quilting with her. Along with the festival came several nights in a wonderful hotel and a variety of meals in excellent restaurants located around the area.

As I think back to that time, I laugh at my awareness of my ongoing frustration with her over being so resistant to unexpected events, only to almost jump for joy when they actually occurred. She returned from our trip to Virginia with a mind full of future "sewing" projects. I knew I had scored points and done the right thing. Additionally, I had gained a deep appreciation of a skill I had never been aware of before that trip. She never did attempt to make a quilt after that visit, but I know in her heart there was always a quilt being formulated in her thoughts. More importantly for both of us, though, was the idea that our excursion was necessary for both of us to actively prevent ourselves from becoming overwhelmed by the knowledge that NASH was slowly compromising her body. In the presence of an irreversible situation in terms of her health, it is critical to continue our day-to-day routines and traveling habits for as long as possible.   I am also working on that for myself, but with minimal success just yet.

Chapter Four
Creating a Family

The reality is that you will grieve forever.

You will not 'get over' the loss of a loved one; you will learn to live with it.

You will heal, and you will be whole again, but you will never be the same.

Nor should you be the same, nor would you want to.

*Elizabeth Kubler
Ross and David Kessler on Death and Dying*

After five years of marriage and no pregnancies on the horizon, Gloria and I decided it was time to adopt. That decision, which encompassed the following four years, brought us two beautiful daughters who provided a bright light and a deeper purpose to our lives. They both were living manifestations of miracles, and they will be so forever.

Oddly, as we worked our way through the sluggish bureaucracy of children's services, we ended up waiting about nine months for each of our babies to join us in our home. What are the odds of that happening? The basic average gestational period for a human is nine months. We took this as a blessing as each one of them became a permanent part of our newly created family. Marriage, in itself, is an act of creation, and children, whether biologically or spiritually brought into being, are a natural expression of that union.

Both our children are now fully grown and married, and they have brought into this world four beautiful grandchildren. Our oldest daughter, Celeste, has given life to two strong, healthy boys, and our youngest daughter, Heather, has given life to two wonderful, healthy girls. Over the course of many years, our family has come together as a rich tapestry of giving and receiving as we have moved through our individual journeys on this earth.

Like most adoptive parents, we fully understood that at a deep and divine level, our daughters are our own "biological" children: DNA analysis links every human being on earth to one another and to every form of life, dating as far back as the beginning of time. Our girls both looked like us (for better or worse) and through a lifetime of interaction with us, they came to share most of the same values and joys that we attempted to teach them (which didn't always work). Of course, we took no responsibility for behavior on their part, which deviated from our wise teachings and which seemed to increase as they grew to adulthood and independence. We just sat and wondered where "that behavior" came from and hoped they would get over whatever it was as quickly as possible. To this day, my viewpoint remains the same: I continue to wonder about where "that" behavior came from; surely not from Gloria or me, but most likely from Gloria (if an explanation becomes necessary).

Importantly, despite our knowing that they are our children until the end of time, we never hid from them the fact that they were adopted. Keeping secrets like that is never a good thing; regardless of people's rationalizations to the opposite. In fact, keeping such information a secret might be a clear indication of some insecurity on the part of the parents holding it in. Gloria, from the moment our children came to us, had a story which she repeated to each of them as they grew to adulthood, about making choices in life. She told them, even while being unsure that they could or would understand, about the fact that life doesn't always give us exactly what we want or expect. She explained that Mommy and Daddy had always wanted children, but the manner in which they came to us was not what we expected. For some reason, God moved us in the direction of adoption and moved them into our lives. It was our privilege to choose to bring each of them into our hearts and souls, and we did so without any questions or reservations. They were meant to be with us forever. The girls loved hearing their mommy tell them their stories, and there was always lots of hugging, tickling, and rough-housing, and mommy and daddy kisses shared during such moments. They were ours because we wanted them to be ours.

With the passage of time, as the girls grew older, we emphasized to them that if the time ever came when either of them needed or wanted more information about their births and/or biological parents (to include possible contact with them), we would help them in any efforts they made in that direction. Neither Gloria nor I had any specific information provided to us about their birth parents beyond the date of birth and some general information about why the birth mother and father could not keep them in their care. As it turned out, both girls entered adulthood without expressing any deep concerns or issues about their birth circumstances.

Our youngest daughter did allude to an interest in that direction from time-to-time, especially when she was irritated with us for our placing her on restriction for some indiscretion. As I stated, we know that it is natural for adopted children to have questions about their biological parents. We also knew that "not knowing" is something that can cause a certain amount of anxiety and/or curiosity in children who have been adopted. I myself know about such issues because I was, at the age of nine months old, taken in by extended members of my own maternal birth family to be raised and eventually adopted by them.

At any rate, it is common knowledge that technology in issues of ancestry has become well-developed and is accessible to anyone who is interested in it. Our youngest daughter, Heather, as a full-grown woman and mother, finally expressed a curiosity to "know" about her biological birth family, not because she was irritated with us but because the urge on her part represented a natural need to do so. Gloria and I, without reservation, encouraged her to go through the process and see what she could find. As we expected, she got a "hit".

Subsequently, she ended up having interactions, through phone calls and texting, with both her biological mother and father, who had been separated from one another for many years. Her contacts with them were both cordial and insightful for her, and over a period of time she decided her curiosity was fulfilled and further contact was not something she would pursue. Gloria and I were happy that she had gained some closure about the beginnings of her life before she was born into ours.

Our oldest daughter, Celeste, on the other hand, never expressed any ongoing interest in the direction of her birth parents, and her decision not to explore in that direction was equally acceptable to us. We made sure she knew we would honor whatever choice she made. Even now, I will continue to support both my children, in whatever their minds tell them must be done-one way or the other.

I should also mention here that in talking about adoption, some people seem to place emphasis on the need to know from a medical history basis. That, I suppose, is a good reason. However, Gloria and I had reservations about it because when relevant medical concerns are present, they should be provided to potential adoptive parents during the actual ongoing process of adoption. And, finally, many of those of us who have been adopted have at least a small curiosity about what our birth parents might have actually been like simply as humans.

Even in situations where contact is made, there is no real "knowing" of what life with them might have been like because it did not happen. Questions focusing on what they looked like, do I look like them or act like them, have a way of surfacing. Basically, if the desire to pursue such questions arises, people should just go for it with an open mind and an active awareness that what might be found may offer both positive and negative insights. One must try to expect the unexpected. I should mention here that Gloria grew up with three brothers, one of whom was adopted.

I could go on forever about watching our children grow up and then create families of their own, but I won't. What I will say is that our children were the true loves of our lives and continue to be a "saving grace" in my life. Without realizing it or intending it, my daughters have served to keep me moving forward in my life (even in my worst moments) following losing Gloria. Plus, my grandchildren are the "icing on the cake," and, not surprisingly, all of them love big gobs of icing and cake, too.

***

Gloria, in regards to our children growing up, had her favorite memories, and I have mine. One of mine relates to telling people that, in the course of our daughter's high school years, they were nominated for homecoming queen a total of seven times. And of those seven times, my youngest daughter, Heather, was crowned one time as Queen. This happened in her senior year. In addition, both girls were leaders in the school they attended, and they were both good (questionable) students, for the most part, and participated in a never-ending string of "school" functions: too many at times for our liking.

For better or worse, they were both very "social" in terms of their relationships with age peers. Their interactions with their friends, from time to time, caused us concern as they gradually grew more independent and actively strayed from our influence over their behavior. Increasing independency, though, was something their mother and I emphasized to them from the beginning, although doing so came with a certain amount of anxiety on our part.

We wanted self-sufficient girls and emphasized to them that they, girls, just as much as boys, could run the show. There was no female category they had to fit into. I suppose you could say that our approach was, for some, controversial due to both of them growing up in a conservative America and living in a consistently conservative Central Texas, and Gloria being from a traditional Mexican-American cultural background. We tried to teach our daughters to be accepting and forgiving, within reason, of the behavior of those around them and to see every person as being special and unique. Most importantly, we taught them not only to be leaders but also to be servants to those in need (which equates to all living beings). Such teachings have become strengths for them in their adult lives. And I have to add here that being a servant to others is highly frowned upon in many American social circles. Rugged Americans seem to look down on the idea of being servants for anyone. We taught them that being a servant to others is of the highest calling and to live in a world of diversity is one of the most challenging aspects of life they might ever encounter. And, of course, both of our girls have undergone the basic trials and tribulations of life, and both of them have managed to stay afloat in a world of unpredictability.

***

I would be remiss if I failed to mention here that after our girls had fully grown to adulthood and left our nest, Gloria and I decided it was time for us to reach out and help someone in need. We didn't actually plan the circumstances to which we were reacting, they just presented themselves to Gloria in her work as a teacher.

Because Gloria was fluent in the Spanish language, she was employed in a school setting that focused on Spanish-speaking children, many of whom were born to illegal immigrants. Life can be very difficult for families living in our country without legal status. Abject poverty and fear can be overwhelming to both the parents and their children, and issues of not having enough food to eat or access to basic necessities is an ongoing problem.

Many of the children in Gloria's classes did not speak nor understand English, making educational goals difficult to impossible to reach. She was deeply invested in seeing her students succeed in the educational system, and she often gave of herself to a degree that was considered above and beyond normal expectations. Most teachers, at least in my opinion, and in knowing some of Gloria's circle of teacher friends, are very devoted to their students. Gloria was, without question, a leader in that category of dedication.

As it turned out, one particular seven-year-old girl, for some obscure reason, fell under Gloria's watchful eye. The girl and her mother were living in sub-standard conditions and were barely able to make ends meet. By sub-standard, I mean utterly horrible. The mother was not married and was working in any job that was available to her. Breakfast and lunch meals during the school week were provided to students through the school meal program, but food availability after school and on weekends was another problem.

Gradually, over some time, Gloria became acquainted with this girl's mother and learned about the ongoing difficulties she was facing involving raising her child in a safe and healthy environment. One afternoon, quite unexpectedly, the girl's mother inquired of Gloria as to whether she would be willing to help her raise her daughter. This inquiry was way beyond anything Gloria had ever experienced in her career. Without giving the mother a yes or no, she brought the question to me, and we sat down and began a deep discussion about whether or not we would or could offer our home to this little girl.

I was resistant to the idea at first. Being a psychologist and having strict rules revolving around client/therapist relationship issues was foremost in my mind. Gloria, being a teacher, did not have to answer to the same types of ethical demands that I was concerned with. However, she did have to consider the fact that the situation far exceeded what could be considered a normal interaction between a student and a teacher. Gloria's job was to educate students, not to raise them. We realized that if we made a commitment to this little girl, our hearts would be forever intermingled with hers. We also knew, being as old as she was, almost seven, that she was already fully and completely bonded with her mother, and that relationship could not or should not ever be broken.

To make a long story short, after lengthy discussions about what to do, we agreed to move her into our home. We also agreed that her mother was always welcomed in our home but she could not, under any circumstances, live with us. We set strict rules as to what we expected from the mother in regards to her behavior when visiting with us and what we could accept as to her timing of comings and goings: showing up unexpectedly would not be acceptable. Also, we talked at length about our decision with both of our daughters. They, too, had many concerns about us adding a child to our home, taking on responsibilities that we, supposedly, had already addressed and fulfilled. Eventually, though, they agreed that it was a decision only we could make, and they would support us in any they could. The bottom line is that that little girl moved into our home and lived with us, off and on, for ten years. We did, from time to time, have disagreements with her mother about various issues (which are not important for the purposes of this book). Still, our life with her, and her life with us, turned out to be a beautiful experience and full of surprises (not all of which were wanted), which added more lasting memories and a lifetime of sharing and being together for each other, as she grew to adulthood, married, and created her own family. I would like to share two stories about her time with us, which have always stayed close to my heart and mind.

Nowadays, I refer to this grown woman as my half-daughter, and I enjoy explaining to others how she came to be a part of our family. One thing I remember well is that she never seemed to stop talking. Talk, talk, talk, on a never-ending basis. Luckily (and humorously as well), she talked more with Gloria than she did with me. Gab, gab, gab. It went on forever. I really did believe she could have a discussion with a rock or a tree without any hesitation or recognition that they would not talk back. When at home, she would frequently tag along with Gloria, attached at the hip, and talk a mile a minute.

I think she was less likely to talk with me in that way because I was less inclined to listen as she went on and on. I had the knack for conveniently finding something "important" to do and quietly escaping. Gloria, whom she called mom (yes, she did call me dad), would make eye contact with me as I slowly receded into the background, her response being a quiet rolling of the eyes and a quizzical look fleeting across her face.

One of my favorite recollections of these incessant talking bouts involved times when Gloria would sit down to relax in one of our recliners in the living room. Before she could blink an eye, she would realize that sitting next to her, perched on the arm of the recliner, our half-daughter would appear as though a parakeet on a swing. She would cross her legs at the ankles, lean softly on Gloria's shoulder, and begin talking. It would sometimes go on for a half-hour to forty-five minutes or more, and Gloria, to my amazement and wonderment, would listen but never say a word. She never said, "That's it," or "This is enough." And, unlike me, she never tried to quietly disappear from the room. She just sat calmly and listened while I, on the other hand, stood (or hid) in a nearby room, trying to keep myself from laughing too loudly.

A great and simple story revealing the magic of how

that little girl, her name was Debanhi (De-baa-knee), slowly worked her way into our hearts, teaching us about love and the idea of endless boundaries. It is sometimes difficult to open oneself to the world around us, offering love and caring to anyone whom we might come in contact with. Gloria and I were always special in that way. We would give freely to others, without hesitation, because it was the right thing to do. I know in my heart that our selflessness was a permanent trait in our relationship and it set us apart from others, serving to nourish the depth of our love for one another: deep and endless in its expression.

The second story I want to relate here involves an incident that occurred when Gloria and I decided we would go to the state of Washington for a visit with my biological father and his wife and introduce them to our new "half-daughter." During that visit we decided to take a day trip to Victoria-British Columbia, in Canada. The trip took place shortly after the horror of 9-11, and our borders had become locked down to anyone not possessing the appropriate paperwork for leaving or entering the United States.

Passports were required for any travel outside the country, and we had left ours at home, sitting in a drawer. We did, however, have our driver's licenses, and Canada had always been friendly and open. It never even crossed our minds that we had no paperwork for Debanhi that would identify her as being our child (or anyone else for that matter). Never, in raising our own children, did we carry any identification for them. Never were we ever questioned about who they were or what their relationship to us was. We all just went our merry way, with no questions asked. We did not mentally process the fact that Debanhi was, for all intent and purposes, illegal, which was something we didn't share beyond the perimeter of our own close family members. To us, she was just "ours" going on a trip.

So, with that in mind, we showed up at the Port Angeles, Washington, crossing station and informed them that we wanted to visit Canada for the day with our daughter but didn't have our passports. The Border Patrol personnel checked our licenses and assured us that everything would be okay and that our daughter, because of her age, would not need any paperwork (just as we assumed). Gloria and I were happy that the passports wouldn't be an issue, and we were excited about having a great day in Victoria. Everything was working just as we had planned.

We boarded the ferry and settled in, enjoying a two-hour trip from the U.S. to BC. Our visit turned out to be a fantastic adventure. We enjoyed some excellent food and even went to explore a butterfly exhibition in the downtown area. Debanhi had a great time and seemed to enjoy just walking here and there, talking, soaking up the sights, and wandering through an endless array of shops lining the streets. When the time came to once again board the Cojo for the return trip to Port Angeles, though, we were greeted with an unforeseen surprise. The border guards on the Canadian side asked to see our passports. I explained to them that we did not have them and that the guards in Port Angeles had used our licenses from Texas for identification, assuring us there would be no problem coming back. The border guards appeared to accept my explanation but, at the same time, seemed curious about the little girl holding hands with us who, quite frankly, was very small and a real cutie.

One of the guards, making friendly conversation with her, asked her, "Is this your mommy and daddy?" Gloria and I suddenly turned into a pair of rigid statues. What happens if she says, "No. I just live with them?"

But, to our amazement, this incessantly talking, yacking, and going on about everything half-daughter suddenly became very quiet and shy (thank you, God). She smiled sweetly, lowered her head, and shuffled her feet while clinging to my leg. The guard, smiling, stood quietly observing her. She said nothing. The guard then burst out laughing and said something to the effect of, "She is a beautiful little girl. You folks have a wonderful day and enjoy your trip back to Washington." It goes without saying that we had more than a wonderful trip back; we were almost hysterical with joy. We sat and thanked the Lord for not ending our lives in some obscure jail in the middle of Mexico following our deportation there by Canadian Authorities after being arrested for attempting to cross an illegal alien into the United States. Over the following years, we laughed and occasionally shuddered, thinking about that experience. It was a strange way to strengthen our bond with Debanhi, and it was certainly effective. And it was so gratifying to learn that, at totally unpredictable times, she could actually be very quiet.

I want to mention here that all the stories I am relating about our children took place prior to the time when Gloria was diagnosed with cancer and represent how she and I grew in our love for one another. Never in my entire life did I ever suspect that I would be grieving, as I am now, for her loss. She is gone, and I am lost. My children have been here for me, but I feel I have not been there for them. I am probably wrong about that, but when such thoughts arise, being right or wrong has no real meaning. It is just the ugly present moment staring me in the face. I am just wandering, exploring my relationship with Gloria and how our life came to be shaped.

Recently, during a moment of connecting with my sorrow while visiting with my daughter, Celeste, I explained that during our entire married life, neither Gloria nor myself ever, when interacting with one another, referred to each other by our given names: she never called me Tom, and I never called her Gloria. She did call me Tomas at times, but our usual reference to each other was simply, "Babe." As our grandchildren entered the picture, we became Gamma and Bampo (which we could substitute for Babe). The only time we referred to each other as Gloria or Tom was during interactions with people outside our immediate family. I think this was part of our evolution as she and I became WE.

***

Once again, I was sitting in my car staring at another row of hospital rooms and administrative offices, which towered above me for a least five stories. As a conscious distraction, to offset my depressive feelings, I was trying to decide what color the building in front of me actually was. It was not quite gray, nor was it quite white. There is no way to really describe it other than BLAAH or YEECH, or maybe BLAAH and UGGH (typical hospital atmosphere when you don't want to be in one). I was, as usual, sitting alone because Gloria was undergoing an MRI, and, as usual, I was not allowed in the building due to precautions surrounding the continued presence of coronavirus.

Lucky for me, the weather was almost enjoyable for that time of the year in Central Texas. On the preceding day, the temperature was about ninety-four degrees (a not-good for sitting in your car kind of day). On MRI day, however, due to an early morning rain shower, the high was a pleasant eighty, and there was a gentle breeze flowing through my rolled-down windows, making life tolerable. I was trying to keep my imagination in check as I waited and worried about her being in that building again by herself. My mind was overflowing with racing thoughts about how she was feeling. She had always been claustrophobic about being in closed spaces but had no knowledge of how that fear developed. I was unsure how long I would have to wait.

The MRI procedure, from prep to completion, usually took a minimum of one hour. That length of time ensured that a comprehensive view of her liver would be provided to those who would visually scan the results and then provide an interpretation of what they encountered. Specifically, they were searching for signs of any new cancerous lesions, which might have formed since her last embolization. That information would be forwarded to her medical team in the Interventional Radiology Department, where they would examine the findings and schedule us (her) to meet with them to go over the results.

Gloria never was a big fan of MRIs (who is?), but, to

her credit, she learned to adjust to them. When she first started the procedures, she was usually so anxious that she requested an intravenous dose of a mild sedative to help her remain calm. The sedative relaxed her to a point where she could be conscious and responsive to any instructions from staff while allowing her breathing and body responses to flow normally. Also, most of her MRI procedures required that she be given an intravenous dye to enhance visual clarity for the doctors and specialists searching for specific signs and locations of new cancerous growth. The addition of the dye meant that a nurse would have to search for an adequate vein for the injection to be appropriately carried out. Gloria's veins were notorious for somehow floating or disappearing.

Probing for the right vein seemed to be an ongoing issue when she was getting injections or being prepared for a procedure. The constant inserting of the needle and moving it around in search of a vein would result in extensive bruising, giving the appearance that she had been battered severely by something. For Gloria, the bruising itself was not painful, but the probing was. And the appearance of mass areas of bruising on her hands and arms was disheartening, ugly, and a nasty reminder of how her cancer was violating her to the very core of her existence. MRIs, in her mind, and mine as well, were nothing to look forward to.

On the day I am referencing, however, before exiting our car, she told me that she was going to be brave. She had decided that she would not ask for any relaxants, choosing instead to tough it out. She was determined to tolerate the closed-in space of "the tube," and she would ignore the loud, thumping noises that would resonate throughout her body.

She had decided that she would pray and meditate during the entire time of her scan. After a deep hug and a kiss, she bravely exited our car and entered the hospital.

I worked on keeping my own anxiety at bay by reading. My anxiety at that time consisted of a mild but intrusive contraction of the muscles in my back and legs and a "jittery" feeling pulsing through my body. I felt afraid. Repeatedly, I would glance at my watch, wondering what kind of time span I'd be forced to experience. I consciously attempted to keep my mind busy with positive thoughts while trying to avoid my natural inclination to catastrophize, which sometimes appeared as though from nowhere. As I waited, I was finishing the last several pages of Bakari Sellers' just-published new book, "My Vanishing Country: A Memoir."

In it, he talks about the birth of his daughter, Sadie, and her diagnosis of *biliary atresia* (a liver condition) and the horrible realization that without a transplant, she might not live. I could readily relate to and feel the pain that he and his wife were suffering from, and as I sat quietly reading, I began to cry. It seemed that my emotions were always "off" when Gloria was undergoing medical tests, especially when she had to do so by herself, and Bakari's words tipped the scale. As I continued to read, I thought about all the pain that engulfs this world in a never-ending stream. We are surrounded by, and yet oblivious to, so much suffering. Bakari (I feel as if I knew him) talked about questioning God and wondering about why his baby girl had to suffer.

He also described that despite their overwhelming

feelings of despair, he and his wife did not give up. Through all their moments of sadness, they hoped and prayed for the life and healing of their new baby daughter. Joyfully, Sadie received the blessing of a new liver. The transplant was successful, her body accepted it, and now (years later) she is growing and becoming the beautiful young woman she was and is meant to be.

The story of Sadie affected me at a deep level. And, needless to say, I also was feeling my own sadness and grief for Gloria. I, too, have questioned my God and my faith. As I finished reading Bakari's book, I became aware of the fact that the temperature in the car was beginning to rise. I was perspiring and becoming uncomfortable. My mind had been effectively redirected for a short period of time, but the present was now back and in full force. I continued to wait, and I thought about the many years that Gloria and I had been together. We had lived with one another for a long, long time, and through all of our joys and difficulties, we had remained in love, and we were happy.

I couldn't help but wonder about how much time we had left to be together. My mind and my sense of being were truly, in that moment, without my consent, falling into a very bad place. I had never hurt quite like that before her diagnosis, and thankfully was not at a point where I could project into an even darker future. And, disturbingly, at a much deeper, unwanted level, I was not only feeling horror for Gloria but also, selfishly (at least in my eyes), a horror for myself. Her cancer seemed to be killing me, and I was feeling guilty about how I was reacting to my own sense of dying while telling myself that I should have been focused only on her pain. I was wrong, but I didn't know that then.

And so, as I sat there being distracted, despairing, and feeling guilty, I glanced upward and saw her exiting the hospital door, heading toward our car. She had a gauge bandage taped on her left wrist just below her watch band, where the dye for the MRI was injected into her vein. And, to my surprise, she actually looked good and appeared to be slightly upbeat. Once seated in the car, she gave me a brief description of the procedure, how it went, and how she reacted to it. She seemed excited and quite happy about her ability to handle the experience. She had maneuvered her way through having no sedation, and she was able to calm her mind while lying in the "Tube." A new journey in her personal level of "bravery" was beginning to take shape.

She then quickly changed subjects and began talking about what she wanted to eat. Her happiness had somehow soaked into me and I was suddenly feeling a lot more positive. We considered the fact that coronavirus issues were keeping us out of restaurants, but we had no problem ordering to go. We decided craziness was in the air, and we opted for a meal from Olive Garden: Calamari, A Tour of Italy, Pasta Y Fagioli, Salad, bread sticks, and dessert. Enough food for a good celebration: a Celebration of Life, if you will. Maybe not a good cancer diet, but certainly a meal to cherish and remember.

On our drive back home, with take-out in hand, our daughter, Celeste, called to see how the procedure had gone. As we talked, she started sharing some hilarious insights about how we might, in the future, be able to manipulate my entry into such hospital doings. Things like Gloria walking unsteadily on a quad cane while I, beside her, assisted her along the way as a necessary helpmate to prevent her from falling. Or, I could have her seated behind or positioned upright on a walker, with me providing any help she might require. At that point in time, neither of those options, for either of us, had ever been deemed as possibilities; our denial had kept us from envisioning such a future.

Thankfully, our family has been graced with the gift of humor in our souls, and before long, both Gloria and I were laughing hysterically about her suggestions. We extended our appreciation to her for offsetting any anxiety we were preparing to experience (it seemed like we had to have at least some) and told her we were going to indulge in a great lunch. Little did we know that in the not-too-distant future, Gloria would indeed be using both a cane and a walker.

*****

I'm having a flashback. My mind has drifted back to a time shortly after her initial diagnosis of cirrhosis, to a visit scheduled with a renowned Liver Specialist (whom I have previously mentioned) whose research and practice were located in San Antonio, Texas. We had rented a hotel room close to the area where his office was situated and had arrived the night before our visit to allow us to rest following the stress of traveling for a lengthy period of time from Waco. I suppose you could say we were there to seek a second opinion (although we were not in doubt about the first one).

Upon arriving for our appointment, we walked into the Doctor's office waiting room. Several patients were seated about the room, and I immediately, for some unknown reason, locked eyes with a couple who were sitting together on a couch. They looked to be in their mid-fifties, and the wife was leaning in on her husband's shoulder as though his shoulder was the only thing left in this life that was keeping her upright. They both looked totally exhausted. Their eyes were sunken and covered over with fear, projecting an unspoken knowledge of death's presence. I could feel their suffering, and as it sank into my awareness, a sense of despair came crashing and coursing throughout my body and mind. I was not prepared to feel the hopelessness that rose inside of me. It was as though time had somehow come to a complete stop between myself and them. Their eyes were empty, vacant, and it seemed that we were sharing some terrible secret; she was dying from cancer, and he was dying with her. For me, it was a clear message of the nature of the journey, which would soon engulf Gloria's and my remaining time together. That couple's journey appeared to be coming to a close, while ours was just beginning.

Despite that unexpected, unwanted experience, our meeting with the specialist went much better than our imaginations had prepared us for. We were in the initial stages, at that time, of her disease, and although it was clear that Gloria's liver was compromised, it was still very functional. No ascites (fluid buildup) were noted, and no cancerous lesions were present. There were clear signs of cirrhosis (scarring), though, and he was in agreement with a diagnosis of NASH (Non-Alcoholic Steatohepatitis), also known as Fatty Liver Disease. On the downside of his findings, he indicated that there was no known cure for NASH, and over a while, it would worsen, perhaps to the point of cancerous tumors.

He expressed confidence in stating that she was not in need of a liver transplant, but as she aged, it would be less likely that a transplant would be a viable option. Her advancing age would be a drawback from a medical point of view, as her liver would continue to deteriorate in its function of supporting her body. He recommended dietary management, mild physical exercise, and routine checkups to monitor proper liver functioning. He was quite clear and reminded us again that there was no cure for NASH, and he added that the myths of the liver healing itself were misleading and misunderstood. He also offered us a ray of hope by stating that liver research is an ongoing process and, hopefully, a breakthrough cure would be discovered, although she couldn't and shouldn't put her life on hold simply because of that. His message to Gloria was to live to the fullest while she could, and we bought it in spite of our fears.

Leaving his office, Gloria and I both felt a lessening of the dread that had engulfed us since the time of her initial diagnosis. In fact, prior to our visit with that specialist, she was given information to the effect that it was time to put her life in order and begin accepting the reality that her condition was terminal and, perhaps, imminent. That information was both accurate and inaccurate at the same time. Her initial diagnosis forced us to acknowledge that her life, and every life, is engaged, from birth onward, in a journey leading to death. As humans, we all know that, but we tend to push our conscious awareness of it into some remote, unrecognized place in our brains.

The specialist brought the summation of his findings to an end by telling Gloria that he suspected, based on ongoing research and statistics, that she would have about 10 years before her liver would cease to function.

He reemphasized his doubt that when the time came and her liver stopped functioning, she would qualify for a transplant. I suppose that we could have entered into some kind of dialogue about the rightness or wrongness of her future eligibility for a new liver, but we avoided that issue to discussions between ourselves. Both of us were satisfied with his knowledge and his assessment of our situation. I think you may already sense that Gloria and I were blessed in our relationship together: we were rich in love.

***

Finally, in closing this chapter, I want to make one more comment about something Bakari Sellers related in his book, "My Vanishing Country." Bakari stated that when he was a young boy growing up, his grandmother had advice for him about tough times in life. She lovingly told him, "You can't fall off the floor." I personally had never heard that saying before, but when I read it, it resonated within my soul and became something I now carry with me as a sign of hope during periods of despair: those times when I truly find myself lying on the floor; a place I still, frequently, find myself to this day.

Chapter Five

Test Results

Death comes for us all; even at our birth— even at our birth, death does but stand aside a little.

And every day he looks towards us and muses somewhat to himself whether that day or the next he will draw nigh.

It is the law of nature and the will of God.

Robert Bolt, A Man for All Seasons (1960)

When Gloria was feeling well one of her favorite activities was traveling with our RV. This seemed to be a concern at times on the part of relatives or friends who would ask us about what we would do if she got sick on one of our journeys. Our answer was always something to the effect that, "If we can, we will make our way back home, but if she passes away on a trip or must have immediate medical attention, we have made preparations for that, as well." We had set our minds to the idea that we would always expect the unexpected—the wisdom which comes during anticipatory grief.

It sounds like a plan, doesn't it? We both realized that our views were strange to those who cared about us and believed we should err on the side of caution and be very careful not to take chances.

However, there were also a few who thought our approach made total sense and believed we should live life while there's life to live. The fact is, it's easy to talk about expecting the unexpected but difficult to carry out, even when the most well-thought-out plans are actually put into action. A healthy person taking a quick trip to buy donuts on Sunday morning could be in just as much danger as Gloria might have been on any brief or lengthy trip. We both knew that if we got into our car to go anywhere (it could be grocery shopping), there was a chance she (or we) might not come back. We also knew that what most healthy people relegate to their unconscious minds was, by necessity, foremost in our conscious minds. And, as if to prove our point, we had our philosophy put to the test to the extreme one year, following her diagnosis, during a trip to Big Bend National Park in South Texas.

For us, the immense area known as Big Bend was a sacred place, and during one of our visits there, we were staying in Lajitas, just outside the entrance to the National Park, at an RV resort. The park itself is unequivocally one of the most beautiful and most isolated places in the United States. It is a stark desert, and mountain ranges stretch out forever. In the summer, the temperatures may reach one hundred and ten or higher, and rainfall is almost non-existent. Expectedly, it lacks a hospital and many other amenities found in more settled, more populated areas.

Long story short, about two days after we had unhooked our RV and settled in for an extended stay, our truck developed a cracked fuel injector (which I did not recognize as such when it revealed itself). I knew there was a serious problem, but I did not know what it was. I'm not a mechanic, but what I saw when turning the engine on was huge clouds of gray smoke pouring out from underneath the hood. The truck engine was running smoothly (?) but looked almost like it was on fire (there were no flames-just heavy smoke). Needless to say, there was no place in Lajitas or the immediate surrounding area to address that kind of problem.

The only solution available would be to drive three hours north to the city of Ft. Stockton, Texas, where a Ford dealership was located. To get the truck repaired, I would have to drive one hundred and sixty miles, in the heat of the day, through mountainous terrain and long stretches of desert, with only the town of Alpine (a small college community) as a possible emergency stop along the way. Alpine was about ninety minutes north of our RV site, and I worried that the truck might just stop running right in the middle of nowhere, close to nothing but desert ranch land and cactus.

The idea of making the drive was, to say the least, daunting and was exaggerated to the extreme in my not knowing exactly what was happening to the engine. Additionally, I had no appointment with the dealership and no knowledge of where I would stay when or if the truck was being repaired. The bottom line was I had no choice: the truck had to be fixed. After much discussion, it was decided that Gloria would stay at the resort with our dogs, Dixie and Luke, in the RV, and I would make the trip north, through the Valley of the Shadow, to have the truck engine repaired.

Fortunately, we were good friends with the people

who operated the RV Park, and we let them know exactly what our situation was, including the fact that Gloria, who was in the early stages of liver cancer at the time, was doing well, but might need help while I was gone. We made sure that she would be checked on regularly during the period of my absence. Again, she was not having any severe medical issues at that point, but we wanted to be sure that all of our bases were covered before my departure.

I began my journey to Fort Stockton with a pronounced sensation of dread settled firmly in the pit of my stomach. I was painfully aware of the fact that while driving along the desolate stretches of highway, the truck looked as if it was on fire, with billows of white/gray smoke pouring out from under the hood. People passing me were flashing their headlights and waving warnings to me. I would wave back and keep my focus on continuing on. I literally counted each mile I drove as it passed, but more than anything, I worried about Gloria. If anything in this world could be more anxiety-producing, I was, at the moment, not able to think of what it might be. Figuratively speaking, I was lying on the floor. And yet, despite mild stomach discomfort and low-lying feelings of anxiety, I didn't fall apart. I just kept going, mile after mile after mile.

Gloria, on the other hand, was doing fine. I checked with her continuously by phone. She was walking the dogs, talking to camping neighbors and resort staff, and relaxing. Needless to say, at least in my mind, she was a lot tougher than I was, and she was convinced that all would go well. I kept hearing this voice in my head saying, "Oh ye, of little faith." Perhaps I did have faith, but out there in the desert, it was definitely being put to the test.

It has been in moments like the ones described above that I have thought, in some depth, about the presence of God in my life. I am generally what is called a "doubting Thomas," but during that trip, I found myself thanking God (probably from habit as opposed to belief). One hundred and sixty miles later, I successfully reached my destination, the city limits of Ft. Stockton, and drove through the open service gate of the Ford dealership there.

After a diagnostic had revealed a broken fuel injector, I was informed that it would be about four days before I could be worked into the repair schedule. I knew, without question, that I absolutely could not stay in Ft. Stockton for that length of time, so I asked to speak with the business manager, to whom I explained my personal situation. I talked about Gloria having cancer and my having had to leave her back in Lajitas to get to Fort Stockton. He calmly listened to my concerns and then, without even the blink of an eye, he told me they would have my truck ready to go the next day. I could feel tears beginning to well up in my eyes, and I thought I might break down and cry right there on the spot, in front of this kind stranger, become friend, and his staff.

Luckily, it was just a few grains of sand, and I was able to keep my composure. Then, to my amazement, my good fortune continued in that I found a hotel room within a short walking distance of the dealership. I was able to check myself in, get a good meal at a restaurant close by, and then settle in for a good night's sleep. The next day, at four o'clock in the afternoon, I received a call informing me that my truck was fully repaired, fully operational, and ready to go. I called Gloria to ensure that she was safe and being protected by our two furry, four-legged friends. The dread in my stomach was gone, the anxiety eating at my mind had disappeared, and I was calm and thankful. Three hours later, I drove back into the RV resort just as the dark of night was settling and the stars were beginning to twinkle in the heavens above.

Was this divine intervention, or just a prime example of human beings loving and caring for one another? Quite frankly, in my mind, there is not much difference. I have been a "doubter" for much of my life, and yet, despite so many questions, I love to sit quietly in a church, a chapel, or a temple and contemplate such questions. I do believe in God-but not a conscious God. So, the answer to my question about divine intervention was, "Yes and no." (The issue of religion, as I relate to it, and it relates to me, will be discussed in more detail later in this book). I do not hesitate to say that I was more than thankful.

The message I am trying to convey here is that every one of us knows that life can be dangerous and unpredictable on an ongoing basis, regardless of who you are, what you believe (or don't believe), or where you are. Every one of us is standing in the presence of sickness and death every breathing moment of our lives. Gloria and I chose to look at our experiences in life as adventures rather than skirmishes with the dark, ever-present Reaper. We knew that, in reality, things could go either way, but we didn't stop living.

Granted, such an attitude is hard to achieve or maintain at times, but it pays off in the end and there truly is a great joy in knowing that we were still willing to make moments in that short life we had been given. We had committed ourselves to make "moments" until that time when nature rendered us no longer able to do so. Gloria, though, was slowly moving to a point in her life where "moments" were gradually becoming more and more difficult, and I was accepting, with some reluctance, that there would come a time when she would tell me, "I can no longer do this."

***

We had arrived, once again, at the hospital in Temple. Our purpose was focused on talking with Gloria's Liver Specialist about her just completed MRI results. As we started to enter the main building we were approached by hospital staff, all fully masked, inquiring as to our reason for wanting entrance. Again, we were told that I would not be allowed to come in with her. Again, I would have to wait, seated in the car, while she met with her doctor. I found myself to be more than irritated about the situation, but I could do nothing about it other than comply. Texas, at that time, had just been labeled as a "hot spot" for Covid-19. This visit would be the first time since her initial diagnosis of NASH that we had been separated from one another during an actual follow-up consultation. Reluctantly, I stepped back, grumbled under my breath, and gave her an unsure kiss and hug, watching her move forward for a temperature check and then enter the main hospital lobby.

It was raining as I seated myself in our car. The temperature was somewhat cool but at the same time pleasant, and as the rain subsided, I put the car windows down to allow a cooling breeze to flow through. My phone rang, and it turned out to be my oldest daughter, Celeste, calling, inquiring as to what we were "up" to. I explained to her where we were and what had transpired as we started to walk into the hospital. She paused for a few seconds and then suggested that I call Gloria and have her put her phone on speaker mode as she talked with her doctor. That was a wonderful suggestion, and I wondered, "Why didn't I think of that?" I quickly told Celeste that I would call her back and then got Gloria on the phone, explaining what we could do. Her doctor readily agreed, and we were more than happy that I could fully participate in the consultation.

Her doctor informed us that the two previous procedures she had undergone (which I will discuss in detail) were successful in "killing" two of the three small tumors they had targeted. However, the third lesion was still present and appeared to be growing. In his opinion, the presence of the third lesion needed to be aggressively addressed as soon as possible. On the positive side, her blood results revealed all values were normal or stable, with the only concern (a mild concern) being that her bilirubin level was slightly elevated, causing her liver to work harder in its cleansing function. The doctor felt that another chemoembolization procedure was indicated and encouraged us to schedule one in the near future. I should say here that neither Gloria nor I had ever been hesitant about taking care of her health issues (including intrusive procedures).

For us, there was no real issue to be considered and no course of action to be questioned. We scheduled the procedure to be carried out within two weeks, and we both understood that in making that decision, we would be entering into another long period of unwanted, disturbing anxiety and worry as the date approached.

My reality had become, since Gloria's initial diagnosis of NASH, an ongoing, chronic state of anxiety about her health. It seemed to surface without warning, harass me for a period of time, and then withdraw as though it was never there in the first place. Like other times, though, as I sat in my car listening on the phone to the doctor's findings and recommendations, I was surprised to note, not for the first time in the presence of unsettling news, that I was calm; no surge of anxiety was peaking around the corner, although I was sure it would surface later.

Even more uplifting for me than my own reaction to the consultation was that as the meeting was brought to an end and she was once again seated in the car, she also seemed to be feeling calm and relaxed. We were both experiencing optimism rather than dread. Is it possible to feel hopeful in the presence of terminal cancer? Or were we being unrealistic and hiding in a state of denial? For both of us, it seemed to be helpful that we at least had something concrete and immediate to occupy our minds with. So, we chose to concentrate on the fact that her overall condition was relatively normal (which really wasn't the case) and that another embolization might effectively kill the third tumor (while we ignored the inevitability of future tumors developing and the presence of unseen cancerous growth, deeper in her liver, which could not be addressed). Neither option, procedure vs no procedure, was our desire, but having any choice was better than having nothing at all. We had both learned to accept even marginally good news whenever it came our way.

Importantly, both of us had learned to dabble in the process of rationalization and denial—they were our friends, not our enemies. Our choices might not change anything, ultimately, but at least the fantasy of choice was there. In fact, we were both so fully and consciously immersed in anticipatory grief that our rationalizations were actually managing to keep us from sinking below the surface; they were protecting us. In the end, though, we both understood that we were indeed avoiding and nothing, barring a miracle, would change the outcome. We live until we die.

More and more each and every day, I was coming to a realization that I would have to be very careful in my thinking and my responses because the darkness of her situation was clouding my thoughts. For instance, it had never passed through my mind that I could become a participant in her consultation by just turning on my phone. I spent my whole life teaching people to learn to calm themselves and open their eyes to the world around them and yet, in my own pain, I was finding myself shutting down to life and its many options, all around me and yet unseen.

I want to reiterate that I have had many questions within myself about writing this book. Misgivings, if you will, because as I proceed, I plan to talk at length about my own life, my strengths and weaknesses, my feelings about living and dying, and how my personal philosophy has developed over the years (before and after Gloria's death. I am having doubts. I am sometimes (most of the time) squeamish about sharing what I consider to be my lack of strength. But I want to provide as accurate an account of how I interacted with the world and how Gloria's sickness and death impacted me. I will describe in detail the raw anxiety I have experienced and the suffering that both of us went through during our journey toward her death (which still remains a very tender spot for me to openly reflect upon).

To complicate things (at least as I see it) is the fact that I was a licensed mental health professional and had worked for many years in counseling with thousands of children and adults, all facing their own experiences with trauma, fear, loss, and grief. And, despite my work and successes in assisting other individuals as they came to grips with their own lives, I frequently find myself feeling helpless to do the same for myself. This book is one aspect of my personal struggle to return to relative normalcy following my own death (occurring simultaneously with hers) as she quietly exited our world.

I did die. I felt a part of me died, and that feeling remains with me to this day. However, as time has passed, I sense that I am slowly returning to life. I am beginning to understand that I am gradually healing while, at the same time, still experiencing bouts of guilt and deep sadness as part of that process. I am, at heart, still a counselor, and any healing that any one of us (as humans) undergoes is dependent upon our willingness to both give and receive in the presence of life's challenges.

I have slowly discovered that I am, in fact, "human." I have deep feelings, and I try, as do most humans, to avoid or escape from that which is threatening and seemingly inescapable. I could not heal Gloria, and my grief has brought that clearly to my mind.

***

One night, I dreamed that Gloria and I were preparing to enter a hospital for a consultation about her NASH. The nurse at the entrance was checking our temperatures and asking us the usual Covid-19 questions. The nurse looked at me and told me that I couldn't go in with her due to precautionary measures. I stepped back and told her that I had to go inside; if I didn't, I wouldn't be able to help her; I wouldn't be able to be with her if she needed me. As I pleaded with her, I started to cry deeply from the very depths of my soul. The nurse then turned her back to me, and I saw her shoulders begin to tremble. She, too, was crying. And in my heart, I knew she was crying for all the families who would never see their loved ones again. As I continued to cry in my dream, I woke up, but my crying continued unabated. Gradually, I opened my eyes, and there was Gloria lying next to me, still sound asleep. She had not heard the falling of my tears. I didn't want to disturb her, so I quietly gained control of my emotions and set forth to begin a new day.

***

Gloria's father, whom we all referred to as Tata, as he grew older and weaker, facetiously called advanced age "The Golden Years."

Chapter Six

Surgical Procedures: Pre and Post

I dimly perceive that whilst everything around me is ever changing, ever dying, there is underlying all that change a a living power that is changeless, that holds all together, that creates, dissolves, and recreates...

Mahatma Gandhi

There is a saying in Gestalt Therapy: "The sum is greater than its parts." In other words, you can look at a beautiful painting and know that the canvas, by itself, is not the painting, nor are the individual colors or the paint brushes. But when you put them all together, you create a picture that represents something unique—something that you have created. Marriage is very much the same. You join with one another, and through easy times and hard times, you become something much more than what you might have ever foreseen. At first, when Gloria and I joined hands, it was "Me" and "She." As time passed, our life evolved, and "She" and "Me" became "We."

***

Gloria was a bilingual teacher and lover of children, and I, on the other hand, was a mental health professional (most people referred to me as a psychologist, although my specific degree was in counseling, and I was also a Licensed Professional Counselor). My job, as one might expect, involved working with those who were suffering from multiple problems presented to them by life. While I worked with both young and old, I eventually began to specialize in the area of adolescence, with my main focus being on teenage females who had been removed from abusive home backgrounds. I, like Gloria, had a great love and caring for the people I worked with, trying to teach them ways to overcome the terrible abuses and losses they had experienced in their lives.

Together, Gloria and I, in offering ourselves to the care and treatment of others, evolved into a force of love that far exceeded anything that would have been experienced if we had simply looked at our chosen vocations as our jobs. We weren't cut out for the "she did this, and I did that" approach. For us, it turned out that instead of just doing our jobs, our jobs became our life meaning, and we brought that meaning to the center of our very being. We lived our lives with love for ourselves, each other, and for everyone we came in contact with (even those we did not necessarily view in a positive light). We never allowed ourselves to become hardened or indifferent to those who inflicted their own experiences of hurt and defeat on the world around them. People seemed to know this about us and became attracted to us because they could feel our care. People liked being with us.

Gloria is now gone from this earth, and in her leaving, my life has literally been shattered. I feel as though my heart has been ripped apart since the moment of her death, and I wonder if I will ever be the same person I once accepted myself as being. There have been times when I sense that I have somehow entered into a state of suspended animation—trapped in a surreal world, with life on one side and death on the other (not unlike what I have learned to know as limbo or, perhaps, bardo from Buddhism). During certain "down" moments, I find myself wandering in a directionless void—lost and empty. Thankfully, such moments are decreasing in length and intensity, and as I move through my grief, I am slowly beginning to see that I can still love people, reach out, and care about them. I can still have a meaningful life.

As I continue my journey through grief to, hopefully, rebirth, I want to share special times in our married life that reflected who we were and what we did, and how our actions in giving love became our gift to life. Of course, I am writing from my own perspective. Gloria is gone now and free from pain; she is at peace. I am searching.

An important realization for me, as I come to grips with my own personal suffering, is understanding that in the losses we are all subject to, there may come mourning or there may come grief; they are not the same. When we mourn the loss of someone or something, we may attend a funeral or a celebration of life, and then we go on. Following our period of mourning, we return to our jobs, our families, and the world around us, and we continue living our lives. We are sad at the loss we have experienced, but there is no question that "going on" is what we must do. Our mourning may be intense and may take some time to resolve, but we expect and accept that—it is a natural and necessary response. Grief, on the other hand, proceeds by a different set of rules and perceptions.

Grief, in the way I perceive it, is a response to the actual loss of some part of ourselves that was created when "Me" and "She" became "We." The experience of grief involves the death of "We." In other words, grief involves the death of both parties in the relationship being grieved. In the case of Gloria and me, Gloria died and physically exited from this world, and a part of me did the same. For those who have never experienced grief, this may be difficult to understand. In our relationship, "We" had become something new and inseparable— a unique, living entity that was a higher form than our individual existences. She and I underwent an evolution to "We," and when she died, I reverted back to a lesser form—Me.

Grief, then, is an expression of the fact that whoever is experiencing it has become a living dead person. Simply put, when she died, I died. My entire life was swept from beneath me. I found myself lying on the floor, no longer able to fall deeper, yet unable to right myself. I was breathing, but I could not motivate myself to continue living in what I considered to be a functional manner. Of course, I was (and am) still alive, but the manner of how and why I lived—the evolved "me"—was lost forever, or so it seemed. Both grief (and mourning as well) are nature's way of healing our physical and spiritual bodies. Healing can be an arduous journey, though, and working through grief, for me, has literally been an experience of returning from my own death.

I have realized that I had lost the most important part of my entire life, and in facing that loss, I have been challenged to relearn how to be myself and how to continue living. I am growing to understand that, in a strange and disturbing way, grief is the process of being reborn into an entirely new existence, which is not new at all. I will also say that the children, relatives, and friends of a deceased loved one may enter into the depths of grief without the concept of "We" being present. Dependent upon the nature of their relationship to the deceased, and in spite of having responsibilities beyond themselves, they can experience the depths of sadness that comes with grief. The degree of interpersonal involvement determines the way a loss is perceived. Some people mourn, and some people grieve.

***

I was the Chief Executive Officer and Primary Therapist for a private, non-profit residential treatment center serving adolescent females who grew up in abusive and neglectful home environments. The girls I worked with were almost always wards of the state, either at the child protective level or from the criminal level. Needless to say, state agencies had removed all of them from their homes. Before coming to our center, most of them had long histories of either failed foster care placements and/or repeated involvement in criminal activity: drugs, prostitution, anger control issues, etc. It goes without saying that the work was very stressful at times, and it was often an unwanted lesson in the manner in which human beings degrade and harm one another. Also, participation in our program was not voluntary. No one we served was saying, "Oh, I want to go there and get help."

When our center was first established, it was originally operating under the umbrella of another already established treatment center. That center provided us with financial assistance until we were able to generate an independent income for ourselves. When we reached a certain point of self-dependence, though, we decided that the time had come for us to break away and become a separate, independent provider. To make that plan work, we had to come up with a way to generate enough money to keep us afloat while making the transition to independent status. I guess you could say we were in the process of evolving, and after a great deal of thought and discussion, I came up with a solution. I decided the best fundraising approach would be for me to contact the local news agencies in our area and inform them that I would be running from a small town in Texas to the city of Corpus Christi, Texas—approximately 325 miles away—in a period of twelve consecutive days. I would cover the equivalent of a marathon a day for each of the twelve days.

During the run, we would be tenting and camping along the way, and I would have a "team" with me, including center residents and staff, who would collect donated money, set up our camp each night, and cheer me on. That was my great idea. Gloria thought about my great idea and expressed to me, in no uncertain terms, that I was crazy. She pointed out that the run would take place in the middle of summer (the hottest time of the year in Texas) and that the undertaking of a marathon a day would be overwhelming for me and others with me, as well. But, even though she knew I was crazy, she also knew that my mind was made up. So, after a period of ruminating about it, she jumped right into the mix and joined the team.

In hindsight, the run turned out to be very profitable. One woman, who was acquainted with our center, gave me a check for twenty-seven thousand dollars, with the stipulation that I could not walk at any time during my daily run for the full twelve days. I agreed. I soon discovered, though, that the run was truly to be a mixture of severe pain and, ultimately, ecstatic joy. For instance, on the second day of the run, I somehow strained a tendon in my left knee. It caused a painful limp while I ran. I ended up seeing a doctor, who told me that the damage to my knee was not permanent, but that I needed to rest the tendon until it healed. He wrapped my knee up tight and told me I would have to take a break. I politely explained to him my purpose in doing the run, and that I could not take a break: too many people were depending on me. I made it clear to him that I intended to finish what I had started. And from that day, until day twelve, my knee was religiously rewrapped every morning, and my next marathon would begin again.

News teams from all over Texas were responding to the story of my journey and would show up every day to interview me and talk with residents and staff, who were in attendance and rooting me on as we all traveled down I-35 access roads toward the distant city by the sea. Gloria and my daughters were always close behind me in our car, and behind her was a center van with staff and teenagers from the center. The heat, as I ran, was unbearable at times, but we all just kept going. As I ran through towns both small and large, along Interstate 35, people would come out to watch, wave, and donate money to our support vehicles or to Gloria directly. Gloria had never been a cheerleader during her high school years, but she became one of the best on that trip.

I ran almost exclusively during midday. Temperatures were consistently 104 to 106 degrees. I actually ate my lunch meals while I ran. My food intake seemed to revolve around pork and beans, and other foods high in carbohydrate content. I drank water on a continuous basis and was consuming as much as three gallons every day, plus drinking sports drinks. To my surprise, as the days went by, I began to sense that instead of gradually wearing down, I was actually getting stronger. I began to realize what it might be like to be a professional athlete (which I decided I never wanted to be). There was pain at times, which I thought might end my run, but I couldn't let that happen. On one morning after waking, I found that I was unable to stand up due to my legs being so stiff and sore. I could roll over in our tent, but I could not get to my feet. Gloria, always my biggest source of support, and one of the staff team members entered our tent, took me by the arms, and stood me up. They then walked me outside and supported me as I moved around the camping area until I felt myself beginning to loosen up and knew I could run another day.

Gloria and my daughters were always right behind me in our car, as I ran, cheering me along. The heat of the days was also taking a horrible toll on them and the staff and girls who traveled with them. At times, our car and the staff van, loaded with residents of the center, would drive ahead of me a mile or two, and then wait for me to pass while they yelled out support and encouragement. From my vantage point in approaching them, I could see a whole group of people standing and waiting, then jumping up and down, yelling and screaming encouragement for me to keep going. This behavior, on their part, was sometimes very irritating to me. At times I was weary to the bone and fighting urges to just quit, and yet there they were, merrily hopping up and down and having what appeared to be a great, fun time. I was misreading how they were feeling (they were tired too), and eventually, my episodes of personal disgruntlement served to bolster my determination to complete what I had set out to do. I realized that their support was a huge factor in my motivation to continue moving. I even found myself laughing, at times, seeing them in the distance as I kept moving forward. I truly think that Gloria, once she became fully involved, despite the heat and the tent camping day after day, had reached a point where, if I had decided I couldn't go on, she would rally the team, pick me up, and carry me to the finish line. Luckily, that was not necessary.

On several occasions, we had people visit our group and volunteer to provide us with prepared meals, water, and a place to pitch our tents for the night. And they usually topped that off with monetary donations as well. The run actually turned out to be exciting and rewarding, both spiritually and physically, and brought us all together at a much deeper level. But it was never as easy as we would have wanted it to be, or hoped it would be when we first started. The best things in life require a lot of hard work.

Anecdotes about incidents on the run were common. On one night, while camping in a state park area, a monstrous summer storm rose up. Winds were over sixty miles an hour, and torrential rains drenched our entire campsite. Our tents, and every person in them, including Gloria, were soaked to the bone. The wind was so forceful that all of our tents were dislodged and collapsed, and our sleeping bags were saturated. The following morning, after very little sleep, we packed up our gear, broke camp, and headed on down the road. Surprisingly, there was very little complaining about the storm (odd for teenagers, especially). At the end of that day of running, we set our bedding out to dry in the sun, had a good meal, and began discussing our route for the next day. It seemed like the run was turning out to be a true adventure.

On another night, we were camped out near a lake, and in the moonless dark of the night, needing to pee, I crawled out of our sleeping bag and set out across a vast concrete parking area, headed for the bathroom. As I moved forward, I noticed directly in front of me a log lying on the pavement. As I started to cross over it, I felt something move, causing me to quickly jump away. Turning back, I beheld a good-sized alligator (not a log) lying there, staring at me. It moved ever so slightly, considered my presence for a moment, and then turned and shuffled off into the blackness of the night. Maybe he was full.

On day twelve, the final day of the run, we entered the city of Corpus Christi. I chose to run down the middle of Ocean Drive, past the L-and T-heads, which lined the bay, to end our journey in a public park near the water. News vans and several other vehicles fell in behind our group as we passed lines of cars being slowed by our presence there. I was filmed as I moved through traffic toward the end of my run, to the sounds of car horns honking, people cheering, and the raising of fists heralding the victorious completion of my journey. As I entered the park, there was a crowd waiting for me, cheering and applauding me on. Gloria and my daughters, who had broken away from our group as we entered the city, were there with her mother and father and her brothers, waiting for me to break a ribbon that had been stretched out before me. As I broke through that ribbon, Gloria ran to me, and we embraced and cried together. We had reached the end of a long, difficult, forever memorable adventure, representing the beginning of a new direction for our center and the young women who, over the next several decades, would be served there.

Little did we know, as we stood there at that finish line, that several years later, as I approached the time for my retirement, our world would change directions in unexpected ways, and Gloria would begin her own journey down a long and arduous path toward a distant point from which there would be no return—no coming back.

From time to time, as we passed through the stages of her cancer's progression, Gloria would become aware of my anxiety and question me about why I thought it was happening. This would cause me, as I gazed into her eyes and smiling face, to laugh. "You are kidding, right?" I'd inquire, and she'd laugh right along with me. Silly me.

***

My thoughts race as I now reflect on one of Gloria's embolization procedures: there was absolutely nothing fun about them. We had arrived at the hospital early in the morning for the required blood tests. Then, following the required "draw," we went directly to the IR (Intravenous Radiation) area where we discovered that her procedure had

81

been rescheduled from 11:30 A.M. to 12:30 P.M. In my backpack, I had two packages of peanut butter crackers, two bottles of water, and my Nook.

I found myself, once again, ruminating on the fact that we were in a hospital, in a waiting room, in the middle of Central Texas, while COVID-19 was wreaking havoc all around us. We were (of course) masked up. A definite plus for me was the fact that I was no longer required to sit in my car waiting for her. Now, I was being allowed to wait with others, all wearing masks. COVID had me completely freaked out, but I didn't share such feelings with Gloria. The last thing I wanted to do was pass my negativity on to her just before she was going to undergo a procedure. Besides, she was probably having many of the same thoughts I was. So, we sat in the waiting area, listening to people cough and sneeze as they squirmed, slumped in wheelchairs, or entered the area shuffling along behind walkers. Many patients were assisted by family members, friends, or nurses (all wearing masks). Gloria was still fully ambulatory, and she was not overtly suffering at that point in her treatment.

Some of the people we were observing looked as though they might keel over and die right there on the spot. The scene was like a living nightmare—a horror movie come to life. We waited and we watched, and we were as paranoid as hell. Eventually, thank God, we were directed to a prepping area. Gloria, as usual, stoically went through the routine of being poked and probed, and she was given intravenous saline and a bag of platelets (because hers were steadily dropping), and a variety of cocktail-like chemicals. I was allowed to stay with her throughout the prepping process. I had no intention of leaving her side for any reason other than to go to the bathroom.

Over the years of our marriage, we had come to an understanding that, at any time, when either of us had to undergo a hospital operation or procedure involving sedation and/or possible surgery, there was a possibility that we might not come back. We always believed, without question, that we would come back, but we also agreed that we would never say goodbye to one another under those circumstances. We would instead kiss and say to one another, "I'll see you later." I let her know that I would be waiting for her.

Finally, she was transported to the operating room. She was almost asleep when they wheeled her out of the preparation area. I, one more time, had to relocate to the waiting area and was, unfortunately, wide awake and still freaking out over the constant arrival and departure of what I considered to be "The Walking Dead." I was hungry, thirsty, and scared for Gloria. At times, I would glance around, then quickly lower my mask to below my chin, visually rescan my immediate area, and then, as quickly as I could, consume a peanut butter cracker and take several swallows of bottled water—my lunch. I would repeat this ritual five more times for a total of six crackers and most of one bottle of water. Talk about OCD. Talk about paranoia. I literally, internally, cringed each time I moved my mask upward. I was expecting some weird specter to suddenly rise up before my eyes—the grim reaper, or maybe Freddy, dressed in ominous black, eyeballing me, looking to enter into my soul. As I now rewrite about that experience, I am well aware of the humor in it: outright stupid and hilarious, really. But it wasn't even close to being a laughing matter when it was actually happening.

Gloria's surgery, I was told, would last about an hour. I, without question, was literally counting the minutes. Of course, at the end of one hour, there was no word of completion from the OR—no nurse coming down the hallway giving me a thumbs up. Trying to be the optimist that I am now, and was then, I arbitrarily decided to accept an additional gap of fifteen to twenty minutes for the procedure to be completed. Twenty minutes later… still no word from the OR. I could feel anxiety swelling up inside me, but I was managing to maintain a calm exterior. To others in the waiting room, I probably looked serene. Who could tell? I was wearing a mask. I would take deep, calming breaths through my nose and exhale quietly through my mouth. Alas, I am not a Buddhist monk, nor a cloistered priest; my anxiety was still swimming around inside me, where only I could experience it. At last, at one-and-a-half hours, I became aware of a nurse approaching me. She smiled, told me that Gloria's procedure went well, and she was in the recovery room where I could join her. I exhaled a deep breath of pure relief, felt myself relax, shouldered my backpack, and followed the nurse down the hallway.

Gloria was still asleep as I settled into a chair next to where she was lying. I was told that she should not move for the next two hours. She was lying on her back and should not roll over or move her legs. They wanted to be sure that she didn't bleed from the artery in her groin, into which a catheter had been inserted as part of the procedure. My anxiety and uneasiness had, for the most part, passed… I knew she was okay. I read, drank, and ate more crackers, and thanked God for getting her through another procedure. Again, I've never been a very "religious" person, but I'd somehow find the words, "Thank you, Lord," coursing through my mind after doctor visits and surgical interventions. She was sleeping, breathing deeply, and at times I would reach out to caress her forehead and cheeks. She looked so vulnerable and fragile.

Two hours later, satisfied that she was not going to bleed, the doctor agreed that she would be allowed to go home. They gradually woke her up through talking and poking at her—and getting me to do the same. I was given instructions as to what she could and could not do. I helped her dress and carefully moved her, with her help as she became more alert, to a wheelchair. We left the hospital that day at about 4:30 in the afternoon. The drive home took close to an hour. I helped her get situated in our bedroom and then, suddenly, it crossed my mind that I was starving, but my work was not yet done. Once I felt confident that she was comfortable and resting, I headed out to the pharmacy for her pain medication and an anti-nausea prescription. My next stop was for a medium pizza and a salad to go (for me, not for her).

Once back home and settled in, I ate half of the pizza and all of the salad, and then swallowed down a bottle of black cherry soda (a big mistake following a day with nothing but crackers and water). Shortly after dinner, my bowels seemed to come alive, in an unwanted way, to a massive release of loose stool. I wondered if I was letting go of anxiety or had made a bad choice of nourishment. Who knows? But I felt better afterward and hoped I wasn't coming down with something COVID-like from being in a hospital (petri dish) all day long. I wondered if I was becoming a hypochondriac. Gloria had chicken noodle soup for her dinner. She handled it well.

The detailed description I am focusing on here is a reflection of what happens during anticipatory grief and later in severe bouts of grief, in general. We both somehow continued to function despite an overpowering awareness of the fact that what we were going through was not going to change the outcome of what we were faced with. The details I have offered here are not information I normally would share with others. People suffering from grief often feel like they are going crazy, developing life-threatening medical conditions, and/or are weak in handling immediate problems (or so they think). The procedures that Gloria underwent may or may not have prolonged her time here on earth: we were unable to say or know one way or the other. Can anyone ever be sure?

Once home and settled in, Gloria seemed to sleep well throughout the night, while I, on the other hand, was restless and unsettled. The following morning, I got up early, made coffee, and moved to the back porch with my dog, Luke. An hour later, carefully gauging her footsteps, she joined me. She was hurting but was coping with the pain. My racing mind and anxiety were not yet completely calmed, although I didn't share that fact with her. I was already dreading the very near future, preparing my mind for the next step, which would involve the removal of Gloria's bandage from her groin area—the area where her incision was placed to access her artery leading to her liver. That bandage was secured by a very strong adhesive: a clear, cellophane-like product. Removing it would be painful for her and, in my mind, dangerous.

She was trusting and confident in my ability to remove her "bandage." I, on the other hand, was not so optimistic. I was as nervous as hell. I did not want to hurt her and was as gentle as I could possibly be as I began to strip the tape away from her incision. Her lower tummy was already bruising: a deep red, black, and purple blotch, which hurt me to look at. Her skin looked as though someone had scraped her using a lemon zester on it. Tiny rips and scratches radiated outward from the point where the doctors had cut into her. I had to watch for any signs of bleeding, especially close to the artery. I worried that if I made the wrong move, causing the artery to open, we would be calling an ambulance for a trip to the ER (if she could last that long). To my relief, however, the process went much smoother than either of us expected. The tape was tightly affixed and difficult to remove, though, and caused her skin to stretch, resulting in more tissue damage and bruising, but we got through it. As I completed the bandage removal, I exhaled a long, deep sigh and felt myself calm. Gloria had tears in her eyes but was soon relaxing and expressing happiness that no complications had arisen.

During the remaining weeks of the recovery period, she would consume only soft foods: cream of wheat, fruit cups, canned soups, and whatever else she considered gentle enough to eat. I, on the other hand, would be eating whatever seemed available. My relationship to food was beginning to move in strange directions. A normal diet and my food choices were becoming more and more of a food problem. I was beginning to struggle with maintaining routine eating habits and would reach a point where I was losing weight and skipping (or forgetting) to eat meals. There were times when I simply didn't want to eat. "Man does not live by bread alone," or something like that.

***

I was (and still am, when I set my mind to it) good at cooking and barbecuing, and I'm fairly well-versed with a stove and oven. Regardless of how good I am at food preparation, though, many of my meals have now ended up being "dinner in a frozen package" or pre-cooked home meals. I have always loved pasta with homemade spaghetti sauce (Gloria's specialty), and I could make a mean pizza. As Gloria's cancer progressed, however, my inclination to cook declined. This was true even in the preparation of salads. I'm a craver of salad, and we generally had plenty of veggies around that I could combine and add a good-tasting dressing to. Sounds wonderful, doesn't it? So healthy. Me being so independent and self-sufficient? Well, it's not. My anxiety was (and at times still is) operating in high gear. There have been many times when I feel as though I don't want to cook or eat. My stomach has been uncomfortable, and diarrhea seemed to be with me on a regular basis (not the case now). Anxiety, depression, and a lack of energy interfered with any number of daily routines which were essential to my health. Going through surgical procedures with Gloria and then slipping into grief altered every normal routine I have ever engaged in. My grief is an exercise in the process of overthinking, in the most drastic of terms, everything I have learned in life. I knew this, but felt I had no control over it. I guess what I'm saying is that, as Gloria got sicker, my diet and my eating habits (my normal lifestyle) became a serious problem. Now, over a span of time, my thinking brain has begun to show up for work again, and I have blessedly concluded that I have been reacting to a heavy stress load, a lack of sleep, and a very messy life plan due to trauma.

***

Over the period of the last two years of her life, Coronavirus (Covid-19) started to spread like wildfire throughout the United States and, in doing so, it completely halted the manner in which we were able to interact with our family members or anything even remotely related to a normal routine. Phone calls became our primary form of contact with other human beings. Family members were allowed into the waiting room of the hospital during her last two procedures, and they could visit with her at our home as Covid restrictions slowly began to lift. No family members were ever present during my removal of her bandages (I handled that completely on my own). We worried constantly about Gloria or myself contracting Covid-19, and any social gatherings were limited to the outdoors, with appropriate distancing, until mid-2021, when safety restrictions finally became normal (?) again. We lived in Texas (as I still do), where the winters can be bone-chilling cold, and the summers are hot enough to cook eggs on a concrete sidewalk. We were always careful.

Gloria loved being with our children and grandchildren but, at the worst period in her life, was limited physically to contact with me only. She couldn't hug, kiss, or be within six feet of other human beings. She was stuck with me: Mr. Anxiety, Personality Type A. And, as if to add insult to injury, in early 2021 we went through the famous Texas Arctic Blast. We were without power for a period of eight days. Our living room became our bedroom, and we slept on a blow-up mattress situated near our fireplace (not too close, though). We ate mostly canned foods, with an occasional hot meal cooked in the fireplace itself, between times when we were using it to keep the house warm. And, happily, during that time we actually had fun. We would layer up with warm clothing and head outside, where Gloria would play with Luke, trying to get him to catch snowballs in his mouth (which he was quite proficient at). Gloria, being a South Texas girl, loved snow simply because, when growing up, she rarely, if ever, saw it or got a chance to play in it. And despite her cancer and my anxiety, we got through that winter and were able to create more good memories because of it. I am just now beginning to cherish those memories, rather than hiding from them. Thankfully, by mid-2021, family and friends were once again allowed normal, much-needed contact.

***

Although the embolization procedures were very intimidating as they were being carried out, the doctors were generally accurate in projecting her time of recovery from them: about three weeks, and she was able to return to her "normal" routines. Overall, her ongoing prognosis reflected a gradual weakening of her physical abilities, and her liver was slowly becoming less efficient at performing its function. We were entering a new, more sobering phase in our recognition that our time for being together was no longer certain. She and I talked endlessly about the fact that she would eventually succumb to cancer. I hoped and prayed that I would be able to control my episodes of anxiety and not cry too much, especially in front of her, and that she would be able to continue to enjoy life. We understood, at the deepest most profound levels, that none of us, regardless of what situation we are confronted with, ever knows what tomorrow will bring. But, one day at a time, we could still look forward to the sun coming up in the morning, and to living another day—if such was meant to be. We could still dance, still laugh, and still be together, even with death knocking loudly at our door.

Chapter Seven

Learning About Death

Learning to learn is what experts call the
"ultimate survival tool,"
one of the most important talents of the modern era,
the skill that precedes all other skills.

Ulrich Boser

In military jargon, Gloria tried to present herself as being "Gung Ho" and a "Hard Charger" in facing her enemy, cancer. I, on the other hand, despite my military training, had frequent moments of overpowering weakness and the urge to run in the opposite direction. I found it unbearable to watch her growing weaker as the cancer spread throughout her liver. We both tried to hide our deeper feelings from one another, but our efforts were nothing more than a delusion—useless. Each of us could clearly see the fear the other was facing. We both agreed, even in the presence of our fear, that staying as active as possible for as long as we could was the best way of addressing the unsure future looming before us.

***

Both she and I were lovers of beautiful music, and over the years, we were able to see stage performances and plays in New York and other states. Gloria had formulated an unwritten bucket list over the years, and most of it had been fulfilled, with one exception. One experience that had not been addressed was her desire to attend an Andrea Bocelli concert in person, on stage. Bocelli, whose home is in Italy, generally performed (to our knowledge) in countries outside the United States, and we felt that a long plane trip (or even a short one) might be too difficult for her to endure. As luck would have it (if luck is the right word), I discovered that he was doing a tour in the United States, and one of his performances was set to take place in San Antonio, Texas, about a three-hour drive from where we live. I talked to her about attending his performance, but she expressed a concern that it might not work well due to a chronic cough she had developed over the years. She was worried that she would embarrass herself by disrupting other concertgoers, who would become distracted by her noisy coughing fits. This was a legitimate issue, but nothing (at least in my mind) that couldn't be remedied. I suggested that, for that one night, she could use her cough medicine, which had a mild sedative effect, in a strategic way that would allow her to quietly enjoy the performance without imposing on others. After weighing in on her reservations, she readily agreed, and the tickets were purchased.

We planned to stay in San Antonio for three days, which would allow us to take in the famous Mercado (a shopping area) and to have at least one meal at Mi Tierra, one of our all-time favorite restaurants to dine at. We also looked forward to meandering along the River Walk, holding hands, and enjoying the music and the decorative nightlights. We looked forward to visiting restaurants and shops and just soaking up the atmosphere and the ever-present noise and music that filled the air. On the night of the concert, we both "dressed up." Gloria wore a beautiful new blouse chosen specifically for the occasion, and I wore a suit and tie. We arrived early and stood in a long line of very excited Bocelli fans. The night air was pleasantly cool, and we stood leaning on each other, holding hands, and enjoying the buzz of anticipation that flowed through the crowd. Bocelli's music (in my opinion) is something that cannot be adequately described through words. He, and those sharing the stage with him, fill the air with an array of both new and old songs, "Time to Say Goodbye" being one of our favorites. And on that night, sitting quietly, holding hands and listening, we closed our eyes and felt his words and music fill our hearts and souls. We drifted into another dimension of awareness, hearing and cherishing each and every note being offered. And best of all, Gloria did not cough even once during the entire show. Later, after the conclusion of the concert, as we drove back to our hotel, we laughed about the fact that while Gloria made no hacking, disruptive sounds, there were several moments when we could hear other people doing exactly that, quite loudly.

The Bocelli concert, like so many other unforgettable experiences we had, would be something that reflected our need to continue on with whatever life we still had before us: we did not quit. Later, having returned to our hotel, we felt a deep sense of contentment as we settled into bed for a peaceful night of sleep. The Bocelli concert, and our visit to San Antonio, would be our final great excursion together, beyond the limits of our home. Coronavirus was spreading unhindered, and Gloria's medical condition was slowly demanding more tests and the possibility of procedures to maintain her stability.

***

Almost two years have elapsed since Gloria passed away. There have been times during that period when my grief has been unbearable—times when I thought I would surely die—but for some reason, I have continued to live on. Today, as I write these words, I am experiencing a realization that the part of me that did not die when Gloria died (the part of me that went into a deep, numbing sleep) is beginning to awaken, and I am finding the awakening to be pleasant and, at the same time, mildly disturbing. I also find myself questioning how, throughout my lifetime, through many experiences with death, I never once went through any emotional reactions that could be even remotely compared to the grief I have come now to know. In past times, I had mourned, but I had never experienced real grief. Gloria's death changed all that. Now I am consciously aware that I am "feeling better," and at the same time, I am amazed at how much of my grief has expressed itself through overwhelming episodes of intense mental and physical discomfort. I have never experienced suffering at the level I have come to know.

On the other hand, I have found myself occasionally laughing out loud about my psychosomatic responses to the hurtful things I have perceived as pummeling me. And, because I am better, I can sit and remember, without sadness or distress, the life that Gloria and I had shared with one another. It has been a hard road to travel, but life is gradually, in a positive manner, changing for me. I am discovering that I might actually be a normal, struggling-to-stay-alive human being. Unfortunately, my new insights have yet to last for more than a few days (a few hours in some instances), but I am becoming more and more aware of how I am actually hurting myself because of my unwillingness to "just let go." And I still struggle with the idea of "letting go" and wonder what it is, specifically, that I need or want to "let go of." No clear understanding has yet presented itself, but I am beginning to lean in the direction of the issue of sadness. I am also learning that grief, as a process, is a teacher rather than a curse. That is a hard one for me to wrap my head around. Grief has made me look at life and try to understand it in ways I have not done before. I have understood, for a very long time, that our losses and failures always turn out to be much better teachers than our successes. I just haven't been able to apply that knowledge to losing Gloria.

***

Warning: The next several pages, for some readers, may be experienced as a distraction in terms of how I am addressing the issue of grief. I am in the process of trying to heal myself, and I want to explore every option available for doing so. Please be patient and keep in mind, as you read through these next few pages, that I am a Vietnam Veteran (more on that later) and a mental health professional. I often look at life from a different perspective: don't we all?

Over many years, prior to Gloria's death, I found myself looking deeply into how people cope with the idea of death, trauma, and loss, and what they do in life to optimize their own continuing aliveness. Understanding what people believe about life and death and how they come to their own personal conclusions about those issues has helped me to

96

become a more effective helper for myself and others seeking healing. I have also come to understand that stress, depression, anxiety, and other disturbing mental experiences can actually serve as very effective teaching mechanisms which, ultimately, help each of us live more satisfying, productive lives. Grief (as I have alluded to before) has become one of my greatest lessons in life, simply because I do not want or accept it. I want to survive, but specifically, what is in my day-to-day experiences that can lead me in that direction? Especially in light of the fact that everything in life has seemingly been withdrawn from me.

It is my personal belief that all human beings are products of the environments from which they hail (myself included). As humans, we tend to think that we are individual thinkers, but in fact, much, if not all, of our thinking and the manner in which we respond to life is directly related to issues of pre-conditioning. This is my truth. I have learned how to live through the teachings of my parents, others around me (who, in some cases, might be more influential than my parents), and my ongoing interactions with my environment. Additionally, I came into this world with a set of innate, primitive behaviors, which serve to protect me from certain threats to my ongoing existence. Examples of innate behaviors include the crying response in infants, and the even more defined response of withdrawing from physical pain. Importantly (for me), learning to live equates to learning how to survive in the presence of my inevitable death, and the deaths of those I love. As a sentient being, I am destined to die, and I am fully aware (first at an unconscious level, and later at a conscious level) that death will come for me. Therefore, all of my teaching, and all of my training, has been directly related to the issue of my survival in the continuous presence of impending death. Knowledge of death is always with me. At the conscious level, I avoid direct contact with death through attention to facilitating my individual approaches to improving my life skills (which enhance my ability to stay alive). My conscious purpose in life, then, is to *be* until I can *be* no longer. When Gloria and I became *we* and she died, I died right along with her—but I didn't. In order to survive, I have to understand what I have just written, and I hope what is written will at least challenge others who are reading it. I'm not trying to be intellectual here; I'm trying to survive. So, hang with me.

The newborn baby, inhaling his or her first breath outside the womb, is beginning a lifelong, active struggle to survive (although the struggle really begins long before actual birth). From our first breath to learning to tie our shoes, dressing ourselves, going through school, and learning a trade, we are all learning to survive. In other words, everything you learn, and everything you do, is survival-oriented (with no exceptions). This includes falling in love and getting married. For the purposes of this discussion, think about the fact that everything you are surrounded by, your entire environment, is an expression of your need and ability to stay alive and as comfortable as your personal situation will allow. Your home, your car, your family, your job, your education—all reflect the manner in which you survive. Realize, in that awareness, how when you are confronted with loss, that loss represents a threat to the *how* you have learned to survive. If you understand this, you can begin to understand the difference between concepts like mourning and grief: you can go deeper. When Gloria died, I went into a profound, unrelenting state of pure misery. My *how to survive* had been challenged.

In grief, what is lost is what has become an integral part of your surviving self (like your heart or your liver), for instance. In other words, grief is experienced as the loss of your very self; you have lost a necessity essential to your ability to continue on. In real grief, you have died. And, in grief, I did die. Life, as I knew it, lived it, and breathed it, came to an end. Before Gloria's death, I only understood death at the mourning level. The mourning level was functional in that it allowed me to counsel with and be of benefit to others who were experiencing loss and were seeking help while going on with their lives. Gloria's death took me to a greater depth of knowing and understanding of what it means to personally die, while still being able to breathe and walk upright on this earth. I became a living ghost, wandering without touching. I did not know this could happen. If the reader finds him or herself thinking, "I don't need this kind of information," know that this is exactly the information being needed. So, at this point, let me digress even further with a lighter, less intense, but just as relevant consideration of what surviving grief entails. Another, more direct way to look at what I am discussing here is to, once again, consider the simple fact that everything in your environment is survival-directed (by "your environment," I mean everything with which you surround yourself).

Let's be silly and talk about what books are for. Books serve as an excellent example of the idea of survival. All books, in accordance with what I am presenting here, regardless of their stated topic, are self-help books about *living* and *dying*. That's ridiculous, you might say: all books? No way. But try to recognize that the most obvious written works on death and dying include: The Holy Bible, The Bhagavad Gita, The Koran, and an endless number of religiously oriented works. All of them are directly focused on living in the presence of dying. In an odd way, they all represent the ultimate in self-help information regarding life and death: do this and enhance your ability to live and prosper; don't do this, and you will die. Now, add to that list: all cookbooks, all detective novels, all romance novels, all children's stories, all history books, all math books, all how-to books, and, most certainly, all horror story books. The list goes on, and on, and every book, whether it specifically states so or not, is focused on living and dying. Every book you read, regardless of the stated topic, is an open-ended experience addressing the presence of life and death.

So, let us use cookbooks as an example of what I am saying. It has been said that you are what you eat. When you focus on your favorite comfort food recipes, do you ever hesitate and wonder what you would look like and how you might feel if you consumed such food on a continuous basis? If you do think about such issues, is that not an expression of concern for your health and longevity? I know, personally, of a woman who, on weekends, shows up at a farmers' market to sell visitors bags of her homemade cinnamon sugar donuts. They are delicious. You can't eat just one—and that's the problem. She cooks them at home, in her deep fryer, in boiling hot grease. The donuts are saturated in gobs of fat. When you eat them, in any quantity, over time, you may find yourself suffering from diabetes and harmful weight gain; issues which in the long run can destroy your life—kill you dead. I think you get the idea. The bottom line is that all books, directly or indirectly, are focused on life and death. The same is true for every aspect of your daily existence. Everything we experience, and/or create, is survival-oriented. As I see it, there are no permanent answers in life, no real solutions—only self-help suggestions about how to make living better. A "better" life, in the minds of most, is a life more insulated from death (avoid those cinnamon sugar donuts, at all costs). Importantly, life itself is an exercise in self-help (being alive and more bountiful, if you will). We try to learn ways to prolong our lives. Some of us actually (erroneously) believe that those cinnamon sugar donuts are healthy and life-promoting. Think about it.

At this point in time, you are probably wondering what the hell I am talking about, or delightfully agreeing with me. This is supposed to be a book about love, death, and grief. But try to stay with me in my use of strange examples because death (or loss) endlessly revolves around what we have come to know as the meaning of our individual lives. What we surround ourselves with and how we live each and every day determines our happiness (or lack thereof) and whether or not we grieve when the world we know disappears from our sight. When Gloria died, my first impulse was to give it all up: don't eat, don't bathe, don't exercise, don't play guitar, don't interact with others; don't do anything that served to enhance my survival. Is learning to eat healthy a concern for those in grief? Since Gloria's death, I have ruminated on this one issue countless times. For most of us, we celebrate life through gatherings that revolve around the sharing of food. Thanksgiving, birthdays, anniversaries, Christmas… When she died, at least for me, and my children as well, all of those joyous moments suddenly fell into the category of *FIRSTS*. A *FIRST*, in grief terminology, refers to the first time a person grieving goes through a special holiday, or memorable past occasion, without the one he or she has lost. Gloria's birthday and all the major holidays we shared suddenly, disturbingly, became *FIRSTS*, and my heart, when those times have rolled around, has not been filled with joy. I have felt and still feel a sense of emptiness and being alone, even when I'm surrounded by people whom I love. For me, not only has it seemed almost impossible to *eat*, but it has also seemed impossible to celebrate. I remain uneasy about holidays to this day. People in grief often become a concern for loved ones because eating, weight issues, and contacting others become major issues that, sooner or later, must be addressed.

To further emphasize my point about books, Gloria, like many people, had a large collection of cookbooks. And, as might be expected, as we lived from day to day, we sometimes took her collection for granted (it just sat there on the bookshelf, being generally ignored). I failed to appreciate that, in some way, those books were, at least in her mind, of great value. To my surprise, after her death, I sometimes found myself standing before her shelves of cookbooks, frustrated and crying over what to do with them. They had taken on a new meaning for me, one I had never recognized before her death. Certainly, a few of them, like other personal possessions, would go to our children and to family or friends. But what about the rest? I actually questioned myself about what kind of person I would be if I simply donated whatever hadn't been gifted. I had never, in my entire life, considered how an issue as simple as "cookbooks" could become a trigger for deep anxiety. I had counseled people experiencing similar problems (not necessarily with cookbooks, as opposed to personal possessions) and provided them with needed insights to resolve their feelings. But I could not apply such offerings to myself (despite my insights being very appropriate and effective for others). These issues need to be talked about when we seek to resolve our grief. Never, in my entire life, did I expect to be confronted with such an issue. My unconscious mind effectively protected me from becoming too deeply involved with such matters at a personal level, although in my life's work, I recognized that they were valid issues for others engulfed in the throes of mourning or grief. I, like most humans, avoid potential issues of death just by closing my mind to it. I daily deny death, even when its presence is staring me in the face, in the form of a cookbook.

I mentioned earlier that books revolving around religion and spirituality all go right to the very heart of the matter of life and death, and how we are to live in the presence of loss. Interestingly, though, many of these strongly practiced belief systems attempt to offset the idea of death by suggesting, inferring, or stating directly, that we do not die; instead, we transition into another dimension (heaven, hell, limbo, or bardo), where we may rest in eternal happiness, rot in total misery, or spend eons earning the right to see God. We don't die (denial)—we just change form. Also, some religions focus on death as being a transition period in which we prepare to return for another life in order to get it right the next time (more or less). Denial is definitely a survival-oriented word. And finally, when you think about it, most grief groups use books (written material) to structure their meetings around.

Well, if you have managed to stay with me to this point, it is my suggestion that you extend your mind to the idea that music and movies might also be deep reflections on issues of survival.

***

As humans, our personal life energy must be either directly or indirectly engaged with the life energy of other human beings in order for a grief reaction to death or loss to occur. The more energy we channel into a "relationship," the more powerful a reaction to loss will be. The closer we allow ourselves to become involved with the energy of another living entity determines how we will respond to death or loss.

In other words, we pick and choose the souls we interact with, and our interactions can range from extremely close to extremely distant.

My relationship with my wife was an extremely intense love affair, which lasted for over fifty-three years. As a consequence, I have suffered to unfathomable depths. At the same time, my relationship with random dying or hurting persons living in small villages, halfway across the world, and basically unknown to me, may not even impact my conscious mind or my day-to-day existence. I may or may not know who those people are, but they, just as all living things, suffer and die too, but I do not have an overwhelming response to that truth. In fact, I rarely feel any reaction to their suffering at all. My energy is not invested in their existence in any meaningful capacity. I may donate money for their cause (if it's brought to my attention), but my involvement goes no further. This may sound like I am trying to intellectualize the fact that I am surrounded by death (which is true) but am indifferent to it. That would be a wrong interpretation. What is more important is that I am living on a planet, inhabited by some seven billion human beings, and yet I go about my life with no tears pouring from my eyes in response to the natural process of death, which is taking place all around me, but to which I am not directly involved.

The truth is, if I were that sensitive, I would be crying nonstop, twenty-four hours a day, every day of my life. And an even deeper truth would be that I would die from that level of continuous grief. For nearly two years, since Gloria's passing, I have literally cried, at least for brief periods of time, almost every day, over her loss. I have often questioned myself as to whether or not I have gone completely crazy in not being able to control such episodes. The reader, or members of my extended family and friends, may disagree that I am crazy (at least I hope so), and I have, over an extended period of time, somehow concluded that I am indeed relatively normal and healthy. Thankfully, I do not have to undergo unending grief episodes for those whom I have no deep connection with, who are passing every day, and are far beyond my conscious awareness. My defense mechanisms are alive and well. They have kept me alive, in very trying times.

When I do become enmeshed in my grief, I lose sight of the fact that I am still very much alive: I begin to feel, for the thousandth time, as though I am dead or dying. Now, in some strange way, I engage in processing the fact that, despite my history of growing up outside my biological family, and despite my involvement in an unwinnable war, Gloria and I were fully joined in our awe and wonder of the world. We were in love with life, and we knew we were innocent in the eyes of Jesus, and Jesus loved us well. I think about the fact that He felt strongly about the innocence of His children, and suggested that we should suffer them, as they are the Kingdom of God. Stated in another way: children are those of us, regardless of our age, who have not taken the giant step into judgment of the world which surrounds them. Children can fear, and they can worry, but they are children because they can look at the world with wonder and awe. Gloria and I were the children of Jesus. He never told us that we would not physically die, but He did say that our love would go on forever.

***

Gloria and I had a five-year-old niece who was attending, with her parents and other family members and friends, the funeral services for Gloria's father. He was affectionately known to us as "Tata," and was well-loved by many. His body was laid out in his coffin for viewing, and our niece, after having observed him, inquired as to why Tata was sleeping in a suitcase, in church. Her interpretation of what was transpiring around her was simple and concrete, and it resulted in a very light moment in a very sad situation. Laughter broke out among many of those mourning or grieving for Tata, and one could feel a sense of joy spread throughout those in attendance. Tata, according to our niece, was taking a trip and, curiously, had fallen asleep in his suitcase.

***

Humor, unfortunately, often becomes a victim in the presence of death, but on that day, it came to the rescue (as it always should). Those enmeshed in deep grief may wonder if they will ever laugh again, or whether laughter will ever even be appropriate again. But as people work through their feelings and emotions surrounding their loss, there will, hopefully, come a time when glimpses of humor reappear in their thinking. The humor may come in the form of funny stories about living and loving. It might relate to arguments or disagreements that took place but were never shared with others. Healing takes on many looks over a period of time, and when the mind begins to open, the person in grief may have sudden glimpses of the humor, joy, and sadness, which were beautiful reflections of an overall relationship.

It seems appropriate to say here that death and/or devastating loss brings with it a "reckoning" of the soul. No one grieves the same, and in some situations, there may be no grieving at all (at least outwardly). Again, our relationships, and the manner in which we respond to them, are based on issues of energy investment. Energy exchange, and the way we address it, is a complicated matter for all of us. Most children learn their first lessons about death through the loss of a pet, or by seeing an animal lying dead on the side of a road. I have known countless adults (including

107

myself and Gloria) who have experienced deep sorrow and grief over the loss of a family pet. The manner in which each of us addresses issues of death and loss is initially learned through the teachings of our parents and loved ones, often long before we are aware of what it is that we are being taught.

To end this chapter, I would like to briefly return to the idea that everything we surround ourselves with is an integral part of our ability to survive: the recliner we relax in, the table we take our meals at, the old worn-out shoes we wear, and the books we read, are all objects to be revered; they are essential to our being. In times of grief, all relationships, with sentient beings or the things we cherish, become challenged; everything takes on a different meaning. And, importantly, one must remember that "one human's trash is another human's treasure."

Chapter Eight
No Stranger to Death

You can kiss your family and friends goodbye and put miles between you,
but at the same time you carry them with you in your heart,
your mind, your stomach,
because you do not just live in a world but a world lives in you.

Frederich Buechner, Telling the Truth

One of the requirements I encountered along the way to obtaining my licenses to provide therapy to patients was to undergo several sessions of psychotherapy with a licensed professional therapist. It was essential to my own future practice that I understood the difficulties involved in sitting with a stranger and sharing some of the most intimate moments of my life with him or her. I had to be aware, within myself, of what I was willing to share and what I was intent on keeping hidden, as well as my reasons for doing so. Entering into a therapeutic relationship is a difficult process. We want answers, but we often attempt to avoid confronting the issues within ourselves that might be impacting our ability to function more effectively. Every human being has issues, whether they want to admit it or not. Over time, as I gradually opened my soul, I began to reveal a world of self-doubt, insecurity, and sadness related to my early childhood experiences of being abandoned by my biological parents, growing up with relatives who loved me but, at times, were unsure of how committed they could be to me in light of the repeated appearances of my biological mother, and my experiences with unexpected deaths over the course of becoming an adult.

I entered the therapeutic situation willingly, believing it would deepen my understanding of the people who, in later life, I would attempt to assist in exploring themselves as they sought answers about how to develop more satisfying, more productive ways of coping with difficult situations. I opened myself to scrutiny and shared many aspects of my early years, which I had never really talked about with anyone other than Gloria—things I had kept within myself simply because they were no one else's business. As my time in therapy gradually came to an end, my therapist indicated to me that in his years of counseling, he had rarely interacted with patients who had experienced as much trauma as I had. I did not verbally acknowledge his insight, but over the ensuing years, I have considered his message and incorporated it into my professional (and non-professional) interactions with those I have interacted with.

Trauma is in the eye of the beholder. Over many years, I have come to the conclusion that my personal experiences with trauma have done much more to shape my therapeutic skills than did my formal education. My understanding of the value of my experiences came slowly, subject to my gradual maturing as I grew to adulthood and chose the direction I wanted my life to proceed in. In the following pages, I will share with you a few specific traumatic events I encountered to assist you in understanding how I approach issues of loss, and how each of us reacts physically and emotionally when loss occurs.

Grief, whether we have thought about it or not, is an ongoing, often unconscious, part of being human. We have expectations, we love, we lose, and we move on in life. The act of surviving demands that we continue, even when it seems impossible to do so. As I stated in the previous chapter, our ability to move forward in the presence of traumatic events is dependent upon the degree of energy we have invested in any given relationship. As I describe moments of trauma I underwent, I will discuss how I responded to them as a child and a young adult, being raised by extended family members who responded to life in their own unique way. Keep in mind that we are all products of our environment. I can say, without hesitation, that by the time I graduated from high school, I had become well-versed in witnessing issues of personal trauma, sadness, and death. Death was no stranger to me, and my exposure to it, without any clear recognition of it, paved the way for me in the manner in which I approached life. I want to discuss death in this manner because on the day that Gloria died, a part of me (as I have previously stated, many times) died with her. In my entire life, despite my history, I had never experienced anything as personally traumatic as her passing.

***

I will say that as I was growing up and moving toward adulthood, there was the usual and expected passing of great-grandparents, grandparents, friends, and distant relatives. I experienced no severe trauma or grief in any of

111

those situations. I did become sad, and I briefly mourned at times, but I experienced no significant disturbance to my being; nor did any of my immediate family members. Those incidents were viewed as sad, but normal. We said our goodbyes and went on. Or at least, we thought we did.

When I was about eleven or twelve years of age, playing summer little league baseball in Southern California, my knowledge of death suddenly, and horrifically, took on a new meaning for me. During one particular game, we were playing on a field located outside of the city limits. The baseball field was built into a surrounding area of unoccupied land and was accessed by crossing a set of railroad tracks, which lay just beyond the outfield. From home plate, one could look out for miles in any direction. The land was flat, and there was nothing but sunburnt wheat fields and a row of telephone poles extending to the horizon. It was (or at least it seemed to be) a very quiet, very safe place. It was late afternoon, after school and normal workday hours, as family members and friends arrived at the ball field to watch us play, and team members began pre-game warmups. During our practice drills, we all became aware of a station wagon sitting on the railroad tracks at the crossing leading into the parking area. We could hear its horn blaring, and the car was not moving. Then, without any warning, that car was slammed into by a freight train, which was roaring down the tracks.

The car literally exploded into chunks and pieces right before our eyes. The car's engine shot straight up into the air, and inside that car were five children and their mother and father. One of those children was a friend of mine, and a member of our team. He, three of his siblings, and his mother and father were killed that day. Pieces of their bodies were literally strewn everywhere.

My parents, the parents of my teammates, and many other adults attending the game, who were just getting settled into the stands, somehow managed to contain those of us who were already on the ball field. Children who were seated in the bleachers were given firm instructions to remain where they were. Many of the adults were tearing up or outright crying but maintaining a certain control over themselves. While several grownups stayed with the children and ballplayers, others rushed on foot to the grisly scene. Ambulances and police cars slowly began streaming in, and over time, the bodies, and pieces of bodies, were taken away, the tracks were cleared, and our ballgame was called off. Everyone went home.

As an adult, thinking back to that terrible accident, I realize that despite the carnage spread out before the entire group of ballplayers and spectators, neither I nor any of my teammates demonstrated any real, observable emotional reaction to what had just taken place. I remember having a mild sense of fright, especially watching the adults around me as they reacted to the situation, but other than that, it seemed like I was more curious than traumatized. Perhaps it was my age and the constraints that come with expressing emotions in front of other boys—I don't know. However, despite my lack of emotion, I can say that that event has remained firmly entrenched in my mind, to this day.

Several days later, after listening to endless news

reports about the loss of life in that terrible accident, all of my teammates, our families and friends, and a large number of people I didn't know, sat quietly during services held at the funeral home, attended the burial service, and then went on with our lives. The tragedy of that incident stayed with me, but it did not seem to overpower me or shake me to my core (at least not at a conscious level) in any noticeable way. At that age, my awareness of the concept of the unconscious mind, and the idea of trauma and stress, was limited to nonexistent. In later years, though, I came to understand that something must have changed within me about life in general. But back then, I just went on living and doing. I didn't have a sense of any real harm taking shape within me. "Accidents happen and we go on," said my parents—it was a part of life. A few months after that train wreck, however, another, even more personal, tragedy seemed to rise up from nowhere.

It is important for me to mention here, as I relate a second incident involving death, that I was an adopted child. While I have discussed this in an earlier chapter to some degree, I need to briefly focus on the fact that adoption, in its own right, whether you choose to accept it or not, is a form of loss, which can result in both trauma and grief. Adoption is a form of loss. How and when possible reactions to such losses will occur is determined by many factors (not to be discussed here). My being adopted, though, is important for understanding the details of the next incident I will describe. At the age of twelve, I was formally adopted by my maternal aunt and her husband, and my last name became Burkig (it had been Ball). I had lived with them for all but the first nine months of my life.

I have no recollection of ever having lived with my biological parents, but because they were related to my adoptive parents, I did have an ongoing knowledge of them. Apparently, when I reached nine months of age, my biological parents came to the conclusion that they could no longer remain in a relationship with each other, nor could either of them provide me with a nurturing home environment. They agreed to put me in the care of my mother's sister (my maternal aunt), who was married but had no children of her own at the time. Also living in my aunt's home was my maternal grandmother, who became my strongest source of love and support. My biological father, once I was "settled" in, went completely off the grid (out of the picture), and my biological mother was "out there, somewhere," engaging in relationships and having children (lots of them).

Over the years, she would sometimes, always unexpectedly, show up for a visit, bringing with her my half-brothers and half-sisters, none of whom I really knew. My biological mother was a stranger to me, but she seemed to have a need to let me know that she was my "mother." She was probably suffering from some form of a grief complex. Her efforts to enlighten me about her love for me were fruitless—I wasn't interested. In fact, I didn't really like her. She was too tense, smoked incessantly, and was loud. The family I considered to be my own was that of my aunt, my uncle, and my grandmother. I was their first child, and I was doted upon. Over the years, my new family grew to include two female cousins, whom I considered to be my sisters.

As it turns out, one day, with no warning, my biological mother arrived at our house with two or three of my half-siblings, plus a new half-sibling who was about five or six months old (none of whom I had had any relationship with). My aunt and uncle had a sufficiently sized house for meeting our needs, but it certainly wasn't big enough for the additional four or five people who suddenly showed up. Plus, there was no baby crib available. The baby's sleeping arrangement became a cleaned-out drawer in a chest of drawers located in my bedroom. The drawer was propped up to level it out and, of course, it was not closed when the baby was lying or sleeping in it.

One morning (or maybe it was afternoon) during the visit, my sisters and I were playing and chasing one another through the house. I had taken off at a run down the hallway leading into my bedroom, with my sisters in hot pursuit, yelling and giggling. I dashed into my room and went straight to the makeshift bed/drawer to say hello to my baby half-brother. Peering down into the makeshift bed, however, what I saw was a massive amount of blood and a piece of thin plastic covering the baby's head. His face had a waxy bluish tone to it, and he was not moving. My sisters, who also saw this ugly scene, started screaming and yelling for help. Both my aunt and my biological mother rushed into the room at the same time, and my biological mother began screaming and crying hysterically. She scooped the baby up into her arms and ran out of the house into the front yard. An ambulance arrived, and healthcare workers did whatever they could under such circumstances, and eventually, they officially declared that he, my baby half-brother, was dead.

After the initial chaos of the death had finally begun to subside, our family was informed that my baby brother's death was ruled a SIDS death (a vague concept to me at that period in my life). Also, we were told that no "charges" would be filed against my biological mother. I never questioned the idea of what not filing charges might mean. To me, he just died—the death was an accident. As I grew older and more informed, though, I found myself wondering whether or not the death, while being formally dismissed as an accident, could have been avoided and was, instead, a "legally avoidable" situation.

Also, over the period of the next several months following his death, I gradually began to understand and process that because he was sleeping in a wooden dresser drawer, and because he was only six months old and had no bowel or bladder control, my biological mother had used thin, clear plastic sheets from a dry cleaner business to protect the drawer he was sleeping in. She had placed a layer of the plastic directly on the bottom of the drawer and then covered it with a comfortable, cushioning baby blanket. Squirming around, like babies do, he uncovered the plastic, which then molded itself to his face. He was literally smothered to death by the plastic and his own blood, as his vessels ruptured and the liquid seeped into his lungs. It was not a SIDS death. That baby was my half-brother. His name was Bobby. I did not know him, and I did not cry for him. I can say that I briefly teared up in response to other family members who were crying, and maybe, for the first time in my life, I felt a deep, conscious sadness that life could end in such a sudden and horrible way. Bobby is buried in a cemetery located somewhere in California. He died, and I, like everyone else around me, went on living. I wasn't lost in a state of confusion. I didn't find myself wondering why God would allow such a senseless death to occur. I was a kid. I continued on in school. I was engaged in sports, and I went on going and doing. I was not grieving.

And, after graduating from high school, I found a job making a decent wage for my age and experience (which was essentially non-existent at that point in my life). Years later, I came to an understanding that following my brother's death, I went through a very mild version of mourning. I was beginning to realize that the people around me could and would die: death was part of the natural process of living. I was also beginning to realize that I was a compassionate human being. I could feel the sadness and despair that others experienced and felt. I realized a need within myself to reach out to others and help them as they moved through life. My awareness simply began to unfold as a natural extension of myself. Intellectually, I found myself beginning to understand the concept of grief, but I had never experienced it—making it, in some ways, meaningless.

And, as this new awareness was surfacing into my consciousness, and my high school years were coming to an end, every evening on the local and national news broadcasts, Vietnam was slowly entering into my mind, beckoning me to enter into another reality.

Like many young, coming-of-age male teenagers, I was feeling a need to defend my country. I'm not exactly sure how that need came about, but as I left high school, it was becoming more prominent in my thinking. My uncle (the one who adopted me) had served in the Navy during World War II. He never talked about his experiences, but I knew he was a veteran, and I knew that I loved him and looked up to him. At the same time, television coverage and documentaries provided ample information about both Vietnam and past wars involving the United States. They also, with great efficiency, focused on the issue of patriotism. I found myself wanting and needing to serve. Specifically, I wanted to serve in Vietnam, and I was aware of the fact that I was old enough to join the military without my parent's consent or permission, and that is exactly what I did. Instead of waiting for the draft, I joined the United States Army. I was ready (or at least I thought I was) to defend my country. I was ready (or at least I thought I was) to lay down my life for a noble cause. After Vietnam, however, as I mentally stepped back in time, I realized that I had no idea of what a "noble" cause was, and there was nothing in my history of growing up that could have ever prepared me for what I would experience in that war-torn land, ten thousand miles from my home. Strangely, as if I was being prepared in some way for what was to come, death seemed to be my traveling companion as I entered into service, and long before I ever stepped foot in Vietnam.

In January of 1967 I took the pledge, and I and a group of teenage boys were loaded onto a bus and transported to Fort Ord, California, where I would take basic training. And, as if death was knocking on our door, showing us our future, the Grim Reaper would nightly move through our barracks in the form of meningitis, searching for victims to begin their journey to the afterlife. New recruits and hardened older soldiers alike were dying at a high rate. I have memories of waking in the dark, early hours of the night to see dead bodies being wrapped in coarse wool Army blankets and carried out of our barracks. Because of the highly contagious nature of meningitis, we were forced to sleep with all barracks' windows open at night. It was winter, and it was often freezing cold. Without exception, the first thing we did after waking each and every morning was to take our blankets outside and thoroughly shake them as a means of controlling the spread of the deadly virus. The word "meningitis," and the daily deaths of recruits from it, were permanently engraved in all of our young minds. But alas, neither I, nor those I trained with, ever cried or expressed any real emotion over the loss of life that was ever constantly present to us. We just went on. Our drill sergeants suggested that we see the meningitis as a gift for those of us who would live through it. It was a reminder that we were preparing to go to Vietnam. Meningitis had taken on a training role, and we needed to listen to what it had to say. They assured us that death was always right around the corner, and we might as well get used to it.

As a group, we were learning to think and act as a military unit. We were learning to support and care for one another. And we were, most importantly, learning that when faced with overwhelming fear, we would not turn and run; we would not step to the side and go around; we would not freeze in place. Instead, we would walk, or run, directly into whatever horror lay before us, and we would die or, just maybe, come out on the other side of it still alive and kicking. We were men. We did not cry. When Gloria died, I forgot everything the military ever taught me.

Following the completion of basic training, I moved on to Fort Meade, Maryland, for advanced infantry training and specialized instruction before being shipped out to Vietnam. And, without missing a step, meningitis was following right along beside me, taking its toll there just as it had at Fort Ord. Bodies were still being wrapped in blankets and carried to waiting ambulances. None of those dying were my friends, but their deaths seemed to strengthen the imprint placed in my mind during basic training. Again, I did not cry (nobody did); actually, I never even thought about doing so. I was never emotional about the deaths—they just happened. And, I was never overtly or openly afraid of the idea or presence of death. I knew it was there, waiting; it just wasn't there for me. Meningitis passed me by, and Gloria was far away in an unknown future, yet to enter into my life. I was a healthy, normal, death-denying young man, preparing to engage in my next great life adventure. Vietnam was to be my next big step.

***

Gloria and I have always loved (and I still do love) the American style of freely living our lives in whatever way we chose to do so. We recognized that all people reflect issues relating to race, creed, color, religion, skill levels, and whatever else might present itself. And as we moved forward in our respective careers, we both came to know many people who sought asylum or freedom in the United States—freedom from the tyranny of injustices occurring in other countries. We also had a clear understanding that our country had (and continues to have) an ongoing need to promote laws that address everyone equally (including those living here illegally). And we were painfully aware of our country's often hypocritical avoidance of legally resolving issues like illegal immigration in relation to basic human rights and needs. We were saddened by the construction of gigantic walls and stretches of barbed concertina wire along our western border—a continuing blight upon an otherwise beautiful landscape. Our country, in our eyes, was beginning to look more like a prison yard than the land of the free. We found it odd that we had strung barbed wire through an endless desert rather than coming together to establish clear guidelines and laws for people who are seeking asylum in our country. We also found it odd that we could and can spend literally billions of dollars each year funding foreign war efforts, while at the same time complaining about rupturing the "budget" by simply passing and supporting appropriate measures focused on bringing immigration issues under control.

You, the reader, might be questioning what immigration policy has to do with the relationship between Gloria and me. The fact is, it has everything to do with it. Our love for one another was founded on the degree of caring and concern we both felt for each other and those around us. We did not bitch, gripe, and complain about victims in need (we left that up to those who benefited from it but ignored correcting it). We, instead, focused on and knew that the solution was straightforward but completely shoved aside.

Love is not defined by ignoring the daily truths that surround us. Gloria and I were on the same page, and we understood that experiencing life to its fullest is an exercise in evolution. We grow and we learn. We were in a constant state of becoming. And, we understood that change was essential to our futures. I knew nothing about Gloria when we married, and she knew nothing about me. But we both learned through our care for one another and our life together, including politics and religion (right next to dancing and good music), were part of the love we shared (not something we would choose to side-step).

Gloria was the first in her immediate family to graduate from college. Her education, in itself, was a sign of cultural evolution. She earned her degree in teaching and eventually taught elementary school in an area inhabited by families who were considered to be illegal immigrants—primarily from Mexico and Central and South America. Her students came from poor families, were often afraid, and on too many nights, went to sleep hungry from a lack of adequate nourishment. The parents of the children she taught were good people, seeking work and trying to make ends meet. Gloria did not judge her students or their parents; instead, she chose to love them. She was as humble (and yet determined) a person as you might ever know. She never sought praise for her work or her caring for those around her. She was a spiritual, loving human being. And, like many of her co-workers, she willingly provided the children she taught with school supplies, clothing, and even food to eat, at her own expense. Gloria loved Jesus, and she lived according to his teachings. She and I couldn't make political laws, but we could live in the love that Jesus preached. Our love for one another could not be broken by different political viewpoints.

***

One of my favorite yearly activities with Gloria's students was to sponsor an annual Christmas party for them at the school where she taught. My role was to become Santa Claus, and I would provide a group of elves (adolescents with whom I worked) to invade her classroom with Christmas joy. Stated more factually, I and my group of juvenile delinquent social outcasts would enter her classroom just before Christmas break and have a mega-party. Needless to say, Gloria's students, Gloria, myself, and my elves, were ready for a wonderful time. I and my group were there to serve them. We joined with them to have fun in the midst of grinding poverty, fear, and the insecurity of life. I became Santa Claus, and every student, escorted by an elf, was able to sit on my knee and tell me what it was that he or she wanted for Christmas.

I and my merry band of elves learned deep lessons about the meaning of giving as we listened to one child after another make special gift requests. And, as Santa, I found I had to be very diplomatic about addressing any gift being sought. Many of the children's parents were barely making ends meet, and Christmas presents were not a high priority in terms of basic survival (although, in reality, they just might be). My elves were informed in advance to be aware of the needs of the children we were serving; not something they were generally adept at, and this was a deep enlightenment for them as well. My elves learned that even while they, themselves, were needy, there were many others who could benefit from their love and their willingness to take the time to care. As Santa, during many Christmas parties, I never once made a definite guarantee to any student's given request. I guess you could say I became a competent politician. And, it seemed that everyone who sat on my knee talking with me walked away pleased and happy with the way I responded to them. Another really helpful aspect of our visit from the North Pole was that my elves, upon entering the classroom for the party, were loaded down with cookies, sodas, chips and dip, and a stuffed gift bag for each of the students. Each bag contained a small toy, a box of colored crayons, a coloring book, and whatever else we might have deemed appropriate for the age group we were interacting with. The parties always went well, and on some occasions, we were even caught off-guard by moving circumstances we didn't expect.

I recall, during one party, noticing a young boy of about seven years of age sitting at his classroom desk, dressed in a thin T-shirt, raggedy jeans (not because they were cool-looking), and wearing pink socks. The temperature outside was in the low forties. I questioned Gloria about his attire, and she told me that his parents were unemployed and that he always showed up to school without a warm coat or appropriate clothing to wear. Gloria (Mrs. Claus) and I put our heads together and quickly agreed on a plan. She provided one of our credit cards to an older Supervisor Elf, one of my employees, with instructions to go immediately to a local store to purchase socks, underwear, a pair of pants, and a winter coat for him. The young boy was unaware of what was transpiring and received his "extra gift" at the end of the party, out of sight of the other students. Bottom line: he had a great Christmas that year and definitely got more than he had asked for.

As Santa, I sometimes noticed that when the elves

started handing out Christmas gifts, many of the children made no attempt to unwrap or play with them. They simply set them aside in a small pile. Gloria explained to me that many of her students would not receive any presents at home for Christmas, and in some homes, the parents couldn't even afford a small tree. The students in question would keep the presents we gave them unwrapped until Christmas Day, and then open them. All of this information was deeply saddening to my socially defective, uncaring elves (makes you wonder). But I can assure you that by the end of our visit, after singing, laughing, eating lots of Christmas cookies, and enjoying loads of good/bad food, we were all deeply attached to one another, and all of us had learned essential lessons about the importance of giving whenever the opportunity presented itself. My juvenile delinquent elves, victims of their own disrupted home lives, were deeply touched—in many instances, to tears. They shared their names, their addresses, and their phone numbers with the children they were ministering to, and later, they received letters from those students thanking them for coming to their classroom.

As might be expected, the very end of our Christmas parties always produced a lot of crying from Santa's workers, who quite emphatically thanked Gloria and me for giving them the experience of helping others. We realized, in those moments, that we were teaching all those children—young and old—that they were worthwhile human beings and were capable of loving and helping others, regardless of their personal situations in life. Not a bad lesson to learn.

Gloria and I always felt a great deal of personal

satisfaction from the way we were willing to give of ourselves to others. It wasn't just that some people were less fortunate than we were, but rather that we were able to recognize that every human being is precious and deserving of unexpected surprises and the right to be treated with dignity. When I first drafted the contents of this chapter, I found myself becoming saddened and crying as I sorted through these memories. I focused on the fact that we would never again be able to share these kinds of loving experiences. She and I, through reaching out to others, formed an unbreakable, powerful bond in our relationship that could never be broken. I miss those Christmas parties, but I also feel a sense of peace and joy within myself that we were willing to go the extra distance. At the end of those joyful days of freely giving, while lying in our bed and drifting off to sleep, Gloria would drape her arm across my back, kiss me, and fall asleep. We knew, deep within ourselves, that we were the kind of people we had always wanted to be, and we hoped that others, through our example, could find the same strength and love within themselves. Still, I cry for her loss, and I give thanks to my God for the years and the moments we had together. And, as I put words to paper, I am learning.

***

At this point in time, I have come to realize that I have been remiss in failing to mention that Gloria and I actually knew each other for only three days before we became engaged to be married. We met, spent minimal time together, and then I returned to Vietnam to finish my tour of duty there. Neither of us really knew anything about each other—we just fell in love at first sight. I offer this information as food for thought. She did not know me, and I did not know her.

Chapter Nine

Reflections on Life and Death in Vietnam And After Thoughts

"Then render unto Ceasar the things that are Ceasar's.

Matthew 22:21

Somewhere along the line, in the process of growing up, I was told, "When boys go to war, if they survive, they come back as men." Those words never made much sense to me. How would war somehow transition me from being a boy to being a man? After returning home from Vietnam, I often thought about those words and wondered if I had achieved "manhood." And then, suddenly one day, it dawned on me that what was being said was that war teaches those of us who participate in it that life is, at best, tenuous and fleeting. We are here today and gone tomorrow, and being a man is connected to understanding that death is waiting, just beyond our sight, and we must continue to live and thrive in the presence of such knowledge. There is a profound truth in this interpretation, but I have realized that such "knowing" goes far beyond issues of war. As we mature, regardless of whether we participate in war or not, we gain a deeper realization of the fact that our lives are an experience in both life and death, and the two cannot be separated. At birth, we are given no guarantees; we may be here today and gone tomorrow. And as we mature, becoming men or women, we learn to live and take responsibility for our actions, knowing full well that death awaits each of us—whether we agree with it or not.

***

I wanted to go to Vietnam. I wanted to serve. And, as it turned out, I volunteered for service just when the war was reaching its most intense period of involvement with American military forces. After I completed basic and advanced infantry training, and specialized training through the Army Security Agency (ASA), I had fulfilled the requirements for serving in Southeast Asia. By mid-1967, I was fully prepared and on a plane, carrying me into a future I could never have foreseen. After landing in Saigon, we were greeted by various military personnel who briefly explained things to us, and then shuffled us onto Army passenger buses, to be transported to an area where we would later be met by members of the units we were being assigned to. In front of our bus was a jeep with an M-60 machine gun mounted on it.

Another jeep, with another M-60, was directly behind us. All of the windows on the bus were down due to the heat and humidity, which were unbearable. It was so hot you could sweat just sitting still. And, to the surprise of many of us, the window spaces on the bus were covered with chain-link fencing. Almost all of us were new recruits, naïve and unaware. One "new guy," as if sitting in a classroom, raised his hand and politely inquired of a supervising sergeant about the reason for the chain-link. The sergeant looked at him, and with a subtle smile surfacing on his face, said, "We will be in traffic, and it is possible that someone out there, along the way, may try to throw a hand grenade through a window. Welcome to Vietnam, folks." His comments resulted in a complete cessation of any murmurings or verbal interactions previously taking place. You could feel bravado slowly seeping out of the bus, with the power of dead silence filling the air in its place. The quiet was so intense and so deep that, in that moment, my own reality of who I was and what I was doing flipped 180 degrees. I suddenly realized (DUH) that someone—a whole lot of someones—wanted to kill me. And hell, they didn't even know me. I thought I knew that already. All those years of living, seeing death, and moving forward suddenly manifested in a new understanding: Vietnam was no longer a fantasy. I understood that hearing and thinking about war and dying was meaningless—until I ended up in the one place where I, or those around me, might suddenly become the subject of the six o'clock news back home. All the talking and speculating about death became, in an instant, nothing more than a reflection of a past that could never have prepared me for being in a seat on that bus. People were going to try to kill me, and likewise, I might have to try to kill them. It suddenly didn't make any sense, but it wasn't until much later that I would begin to ask myself, "Why?"

After being dropped off at the transition point, we picked out sleeping spots, stretched out to relax, and listened to artillery and gunfire somewhere in the distance. I knew that I might have to wait as many as three days before I would be picked up by my unit, and I wondered where that assignment might take me and what I would be doing as I waited. And, as if to answer my question, as I lay there thinking about what the future might hold, someone entered our area and asked for a volunteer. I immediately raised my hand and was quickly ushered outside to a garbage truck, positioned in line with two other trucks. I was given an M-14 rifle (M-16s weren't available yet) and told that the trucks were making a run to the dump to drop off trash and garbage. My job would be to ride along in one of the trucks as "shotgun," in case any problems arose. My mind more or less saw the assignment as taking out the trash; no big deal. I quickly became aware that the temperature had to be at least 105 degrees, and the humidity was so thick that sweat seemed to exude from every pore in my body, soaking my fatigues. I seated myself in the truck, and we began a journey down a damp, well-worn dirt road surrounded by thick, lustrous green vegetation spreading out in all directions. I became hyper-alert, imagining an imminent enemy attack from any or all sides. The driver of the truck told me to keep my eyes open; beyond that morsel of advice, he had nothing more to say.

An enemy attack did not occur. What did occur, though, was that as we neared the dump site, I began noticing a large number of small children streaming out of the thick foliage, from all sides, moving directly toward our trucks. The children appeared to range in age from about five to fourteen or fifteen years old. It was difficult to tell exactly because most Vietnamese people are physically much smaller than the average American. The children seemed happy and excited, almost ecstatic: laughing, giggling, smiling, waving their hands, and jumping up and down. My mind immediately flashed to times back home, when I watched old war movies where American soldiers, like in World War II, were enthusiastically welcomed and cheered by oppressed adults who had just been liberated from the forces of evil that were strangling Europe. "Wow. This is pretty cool," I thought, as the truck slowly came to a stop.

And then, just as quickly, my mind began to reel under a nastier, more imminent reality: the children were not there to greet us. Instead, and without hesitation, they climbed into the beds of our trucks and began eating the discarded, spoiled food we were in the process of dumping there. With filthy, dirty hands, they rapidly sorted through leftover clumps of uneaten bread, coffee grounds, eggshells, napkins, plastic wrappers, and whatever else the camp mess hall had thrown in. The children ate like they hadn't eaten in a long time. They ate like they were starving and might not eat again, ignoring the stench and flies hovering in the air.

The driver of the truck, finally breaking his silence, looked over at me and explained that the children crawling in the garbage lived around the dump site and went through the same eating ritual every time a truck entered to drop a load. Most of the children were war orphans who were trying to care for one another. A few of them had a living parent, or parents, or grandparents who rarely entered the area with them. Instead, they would wait out of sight for the children to bring them "food."

My mind shot straight to the book *Catcher in the Rye*, then quickly jumped back to the scene before me. Once again, my world flipped. Everything seemed grotesquely surreal. And, as all this was happening inside and around me, the sky, with the sun burning down upon us, opened up, and a torrent of rain began falling, drenching us all. I was saturated to the bone, the children were thoroughly drenched, and it felt as though the humidity had suddenly doubled. The idea of a sweltering, steaming jungle became an almost overpowering reality to me.

So much for great, hero-filled war movies and weekly episodes of combat, all of which somehow missed scenes like the one I was witnessing before me. In the scene I was observing, and had become a part of, there was no shooting, no bombs exploding, no yelling and screaming—only children, small boys and girls, starving and laughing, all at the same time. Once the truck bed was completely emptied, the driver carefully turned it around. I crawled back into the shotgun seat, and we began the trip back to base, watching through our rearview mirrors as the still-roaming children grew smaller and smaller, disappearing from our sight. Two days later, I was greeted by two men in a jeep, sent by the unit I had been assigned to.

Simply put, ASA (Army Security Agency) was an offshoot of military intelligence. Our specific training was directed toward locating and identifying the presence of enemy units within our assigned areas of operation. ASA was essentially exploring new technology and how it could be used in warfare to assist infantry operations or other forms of direct contact with enemy forces. In its beginnings in Vietnam, we were assembled as small units to be dispatched into designated terrain to gather information, which could then be relayed to the larger units we supported. ASA units were generally assigned to major units such as the 25th Infantry, the 101st Airborne Brigade, the 4th Infantry, MACV, or others. We were spread throughout Vietnam and were independent to a degree that allowed us to move from one place to another, often times without the knowledge of the larger units we were assigned to. Also, within our units, we usually had one member who spoke fluent Vietnamese. This was an invaluable asset during those times when we were moving through various locations and isolated villages. Many of the Vietnamese people we encountered spoke what we called "Pigeon English," but having a translator with us was sometimes essential to our missions.

All of the ASA unit members were considered to be at the top-secret level of classification, and we generally did not interact on a personal level with any individuals outside our own area of training. We did not have direct contact with infantry soldiers or members of support units, but most of us thought that infantrymen were like gods, because they went directly into the fray, knowingly, to live or die.

ASA members, to my knowledge, did not die in large numbers, nor were we directly involved (sent into combat) in any major battles. Death did come to us, though, and unavoidable battles did present themselves. Our job was to enter areas, gather information as to possible locations of enemy units, and then quietly withdraw. We reported our findings to intelligence officers and others, and infantry would be sent in to make contact with and eradicate NVA or Viet Cong units. When in the field, we were concerned with the issue of being very quiet and avoiding capture. We learned to be invisible.

According to some war historians, the first death in Vietnam was actually a soldier from one of our ASA units.

His name was James Davis, and he was killed on December 22, 1961, while on a mission in a jungled area located outside the city of Saigon. He and his men were searching for the location of an enemy unit when they were ambushed by Viet Cong. Davis and his men were pinned down and engaged in a heavy firefight, waiting for members of the 25th Infantry to join them. Davis had been assigned to the 3rd Radio Research Unit. He was killed while attempting to redirect enemy fire from his troops to himself. It should be noted that Davis's unit was operating in the area where they were attacked without the knowledge of other American units in the same vicinity. Later, President Lyndon Johnson made reference to the death of Davis as being the first death in what he (Johnson) designated as the official beginning of the Vietnam War—December 11, 1961. I have seen Davis's name on the Vietnam Memorial in Washington D.C., and I can assure you that during advanced training, before shipping out to Vietnam, we were showered with stories about him and other ASA soldiers who put their lives on the line. The message we were given was that you can be heroes, and you can die.

My first unit was dug in on a hill we referred to as either Artillery Hill or Engineer Hill, depending upon what was happening on any given day or night. We were located about twenty miles outside the town of Pleiku, in the Central Highlands. After first arriving, I began learning a great deal about how the human mind works under stress. My first "job" involved being placed on late-night guard duty. It was on guard duty that I learned the difference between incoming and outgoing, and I also learned to gain a certain amount of control over my paranoid delusions, which surfaced due to a lack of sleep paired with peering into the dark, thick mist-covered nights. As nighttime would begin to close in around us, a dense ghost of white, cloud-like mist would slowly settle.

As nighttime began to close in around us, a dense ghost of white, cloud-like mist slowly settled onto the ground beyond our perimeter, making it impossible to see anything crawling toward us within the protective shield it provided. I found myself having intense "hallucinations," in which masses of unseen Viet Cong would suddenly rise up, screaming, yelling, and charging our lines, intent on overrunning and killing us all. Of course, by design, I was never on the line by myself—no one was (experienced or not). Others, who had already been in-country and on the line, were always with me and had been through the very same nightmare experiences I was having. They assured me that such thoughts of horror would pass. They also assured me that the "dinks" were out there, and I needed to pay attention to what was real. Gradually, I was able to calm my thinking and pay genuine attention to what actually lay before me. Frequently, we received mortar rounds and occasional randomly directed AK fire; but beyond that, guard duty was usually (not always) uneventful.

As I stated earlier, we moved around in small groups to attempt to identify enemy unit locations. As I became adjusted to my unit, a place called Dak To (pronounced Doc Toe) was becoming an area of concern. Myself and two others were sent into the terrain surrounding the airstrip located there. We were joined by members of the 404th Radio Research Detachment, which was assigned to the

173rd Airborne Brigade. Our job was to silently enter the immediate, heavily jungled landscape to assist in determining specific enemy unit positions. The 4th Infantry Division, whose base camp was located just outside Pleiku, was already in the area and had been engaged in intense combat with deeply entrenched enemy units, involving highly trained soldiers of the NVA. As it turned out, our group found nothing that would improve knowledge of an already escalating situation. The 4th had incurred heavy losses by the time we arrived, and subsequently, the 173rd was inserted into the battle to relieve them. We were quickly pulled out of the field as the 173rd began their own assault on heavily fortified enemy positions. The fighting was extremely vicious, and the terrain being held by the NVA was mountainous, thickly vegetated, and filled with tunnels, making American advancement slow to nearly impossible. We were sitting on the airfield, hunkered down in bunkers, waiting to be lifted from the continuous fighting.

Our exit from the area was being delayed due to constant, heavy mortaring and rocketing of the airstrip. It was difficult, if not impossible, for C-130s and helicopters to land or take off because the strip itself was deeply pocked and dangerous, creating a problem for bringing in more troops and supplies or for removing the wounded and dead. Heavily damaged and disabled helicopters and C-130s were strewn on the strip as well. While we were not directly involved in the combat going on around us, we were well aware of the fact that the bodies of dead American soldiers and ARVN soldiers were being put into plastic body bags and placed in "safe" spots along the runway until they could be transported, along with the still-living wounded, to

Pleiku. And while we sat waiting for extraction, an enemy rocket or mortar round struck one of the airstrip ammo bunkers, resulting in an explosion that quickly became known as the "blast heard 'round the world." That bunker happened to be filled with C-4 and other kinds of high explosives. When it blew up, the smoke cloud from the explosion filled the sky like someone had detonated an atomic bomb, and the sound of the blast was reported to have been heard as far as 50 miles away. Those of us inside the bunkers were literally picked up and thrown, like rag dolls, across the narrow insides of the bunkers, slamming us against hard, reinforced sandbags. Most of us were bleeding from our ears. The sensation that ran through my body in that moment is one that I still am unable to describe, and I suspect that I will never be able to do so. What I can say is that I now live about forty miles from Fort Hood, Texas—the largest Army base in the United States—and when they engage in artillery exercises, I do not so much hear the artillery explosions as I feel them. They course through my body, causing my mind to instantly return to Vietnam—now almost sixty years later.

Eventually, we were able to catch a chopper, and we returned to our "unit on the hill." The Battle of Dak To was destined to become one of the fiercest in the history of the Vietnam War (there were many). The 173rd and other units fighting with them suffered high casualties, and following that battle, it was reported that over 350 American soldiers lost their lives, and over 1,400 were wounded. It was also misleadingly reported that we "won" the battle. In actuality, the mountains and thick jungle terrain where the battle was fought were eventually abandoned by our forces, and gradually, the NVA once again reoccupied it, bringing it back under their control. A sad but ever-present reality in Vietnam. After the carnage of Dak To, the 173rd was sent to the coastal town of Tuy Hoa, Vietnam, to heal from its wounds and be reinforced with new recruits. As for me, I was back at Engineer Hill, where life seemed to be relatively safe. We were routinely mortared or rocketed, but I had yet to be involved directly in a combat situation—although Dak To had gained a permanent after-image in my mind and body.

Once back at my unit, I found myself feeling uneasy about remaining on the Hill as a permanent duty site. Sitting outside my tent, a beer in hand, I watched C-130s approach and land at Camp Holloway. Each of those planes contained the bodies of the dead and the wounded. It was hard to accept the fact that because of the high number of casualties, the body bags had to be stacked, one upon the other, to create as much room as possible in the cargo holds. I found myself wanting to be with the 173rd but not knowing how I would get there. Eventually, however, things would change for me, and I would achieve the transfer that I sought. My transfer would not occur, though, until after I had my first experience with actual combat on the Hill: the TET Offensive of 1968 was about to raise its rabid head throughout South Vietnam.

Our unit on the hill was responsible for about one-quarter of the overall perimeter, separating us from them. Other units sharing protection of the remainder of the perimeter were primarily combat engineers and artillery outfits. On the section of the "line" we were responsible for, we had several bunkers and sandbag defensive positions. We maintained two M-50s, three M-60s, our personal M-14s, and several M-79 grenade launchers. From our position on the edge of the sprawling valley floor, we could look out across the emptiness and see planes and helicopters taking off and landing at Camp Holloway—an Army base manned by Aviation units, a large field hospital, and a variety of other units.

Importantly, military intelligence situated throughout Vietnam was able to obtain information that a country-wide, highly coordinated offensive by NVA and Viet Cong forces was about to be inflicted on multiple targets across South Vietnam. Our "Hill" was included as part of that strategy. The offensive, itself, was to become known as the "TET Offensive" of 1968, and it came to represent a series of battles that ultimately determined continued U.S. involvement in a seemingly unwinnable war—a war we should never have engaged in, in the first place.

In response to the information we had obtained, we notified all units on the hill and then started preparing a defense. We fully manned our perimeter and set up Claymore mines on a berm we had built as a second point of defense in the event that our perimeter itself was breached (overrun). On the night the TET Offensive was scheduled to begin, all of us lay prone in the dark or sat waiting in bunkers for an attack to come. I could smell the dirt and feel beads of sweat running down my face. And suddenly, without any warning, in the midst of an eerie silence, I and my brothers saw a lone silhouette, a dark shadow, rise up from the earth and run full force directly into the concertina wire stretched before him. As we opened fire, shattering the quiet, he threw himself into the barbed wire and literally blew himself into pieces, creating a huge hole, a gap, in our defense. He was immediately followed, without hesitation, by a squad of "sappers" pouring through the opening he had sacrificed himself for, entering our compound, spreading out, and disappearing into the blackness of the night. Their focus immediately became obvious to us: inflict as much damage as possible and die in the process. Their primary target was the area where the combat engineers were located, and our ability to fire on them was impeded due to their movement being so quick and intentional. They assumed positions where crossfire from our own soldiers would result in the possibility of us killing our own, rather than them. Because of the possibility of self-inflicted harm, the sappers, who had not been immediately killed, had to be hunted down and killed individually. But killing them, except for one or two, never really transpired the way we intended because, before the attack was over, most of them had actually killed themselves by running into equipment storage areas and various buildings and blowing themselves and the buildings to bits by triggering the explosive satchels they all carried strapped to their backs.

During our search for sappers still moving through our area of responsibility, I ended up being assigned to guard a small area of high grass within our compound. The grass was maybe two to three feet tall and was sufficient to provide cover to someone lying hidden there. I was totally focused and totally imagining what would happen if a sapper, with a satchel strapped to his back, suddenly leaped to his feet in front of me and pulled the cord. Both of us, without question, would be gone from this world. It turned out that no one was there. I stood staring into nothingness for what seemed like forever. By early morning, the battle had ceased, and we had recovered enough bodies, and parts of bodies, to confirm that all of the sappers had been eliminated.

We shot a few of them and yet they still were able to detonate the explosives they had strapped to their bodies. Most of them were killed by their own doing while carrying out their mission to destroy designated targets. They all died, but more importantly, they all became heroes among their own ranks for their cause. They came through our wire, knowing without question that they would die. They willingly carried out their fatal mission and left an undeniable statement with their deaths; "We will not bow down; we will not quit under any circumstances." Oddly, on that night, not one American soldier was wounded or killed. And yet we lost the battle. They had let us know that we would not win the war, regardless of the number of battles we "successfully" engaged in.

As night turned to day, we set to work rebuilding the gap in our line and wondering about those sappers charging into whatever heaven they thought or knew they were about to enter. A bloody shredded leg hanging on the wire and various chunks of his body lay strewn on the ground around us. That was my first and only experience with an "organized" sapper squad. However as I later thought about it, I came to the conclusion that any violent, premeditated military operation, regardless of which side did the initiating, could qualify as a form of sapper activity. Because we are human, we are all, in some strange way, sappers when we agree to participate in war.

You, the reader, may be wondering (if you are not familiar with the term "sapper") why we would call the attack just described as a "sapper attack." I, personally, have no clear understanding as to how the term "sapper" applied to the manner in which The NVA and Viet Cong carried out their missions, but most of us knew that the so-called sappers were organized suicide squads and their actions were specifically designed to inflict death on the enemy by knowingly inflicting death upon themselves. Many, if not all of them, were high on a variety of drugs before they strapped the explosive-laden satchels to their backs and blew themselves and their assigned targets to kingdom come. Death and love of country were no strangers to the Vietnamese people, and the dedication and willingness to die for their country had been present throughout endless centuries of fighting amongst themselves and/or other invading countries.

On that night, we all managed to stay alive. However, the impact of watching human beings knowingly and willingly blow themselves apart was, to say the least, consideration for much thought. Outwardly, neither I nor the men I was with appeared disturbed or negatively affected by having experienced the attack. We were, for the most part, excited and exhilarated and during and after the "cleanup," there were moments of laughter, picture-taking, deep breaths of silent relaxation, and the shrugging of shoulders. We all went on. I didn't think any of us were traumatized (hell, trauma didn't even exist back then), and I didn't worry about the impact that TET might have on my psyche; all that came much later. I wasn't physically hurt. I got through it. Two hundred and whatever and a wakeup…time was moving on.

A few days later, on the very same hill where Tet was brought to a close, a different scenario played out during a daylight V.C. mortar attack. Daytime mortar attacks were generally ineffective, missing their mark, because they had to be carried out rapidly by the Viet Cong to ensure they could escape to fight another day. Their mortar and rocket firing squads had to set up, gauge, fire, and then run like hell to avoid being fired upon by our helicopters, infantry patrols, or those of us guarding our perimeter; so, they tended to "miss" a great deal of the time. But even in missing, they were very successful in keeping us all in a general state of ongoing, subtle anxiety. This was especially true if their rounds were fired at night when the constant worry of having an "accurate" round actually hit its target caused a continuous stream of broken sleep. Added to that was a deep frustration in the fact that we were literally helpless to do anything about such attacks: they came in the dark, undetected, at random, and totally unpredictable.

In our unit, we had one fairly large metal building called a Quonset hut, where communications were set up. In that hut we had a variety of electronic surveillance equipment, as well as a communication center allowing us to interact with other sites. One afternoon, as several of us were working inside, a "successful" mortar attack was initiated somewhere off our perimeter. The normal procedure during any mortar or rocket attack (successful or not) was to drop immediately to the floor and crawl to, or roll under, something that could serve as protection while waiting for an attack to end. On this day, however, as an attack was initiated, one of the men with us panicked, jumped up, and started to run toward the door. As he ran, a mortar round hit the top of the hut, blowing a jagged hole into it and scattering shrapnel in all directions. A piece of that jagged metal hit the running man and ripped open the front area of his torso and stomach. What looked to be all of his intestines fell out of him onto the floor. He collapsed, screaming in agony. We quickly crawled to him. He was alive but scared shitless, in pain, and thinking he was going to die. The mortar attack ended just as fast as it had started. As we were trying to calm him, we were carefully scooping up his intestines in our hands and shoving them back into his open body cavity. A medivac helicopter was called in, picked him up, and he was transported across the valley to Camp Holloway. He was successfully put back together and sent home to the United States. That was the end of his tour of duty. He was lucky and unlucky, all at the same moment.

As these incidents pass through my mind, I am aware of the fact that rarely (if ever) did we panic or show any overt signs of fear as we went from day to day. Panic was for New Guys. We had feelings, but we kept our anxiety and doubts to ourselves. We avoided openly crying. We just sucked it up and went about our business. We were soldiers, warriors, men, and we were trained well to control our emotions and keep moving forward. We were surviving. Life and death were just that—life and death. As time marched on, I was never anxious or afraid, other than in an immediate moment when there was time to really think about it. In essence, I was learning that we, as humans, deny death until we die, or until we lose someone that we have concluded we can't live without. Denying, though, doesn't always work. Reality has a way of sneaking in and waking us up.

It was after TET and the mortaring of the Quonset hut that my request to be transferred to the 173rd was granted. And it was, at that same time, while being moved to a base camp in Tuy Hoa, that I began to ask myself, at a very subtle level, why the war was happening and what reasons the American government had in sending men ten thousand miles away from their homes to die in a country where we did not belong. I was beginning to realize that we were engaged in a war we could not win and, more importantly, there was no real reason or benefit for us to win. The situation in Vietnam had nothing to do with American safety back home. Our economy and our chosen style of life were not threatened in any way. And yet, there we were, bleeding out in the jungles and rice paddies of a foreign land.

At an even more profound level, I realized that we were consciously not being allowed to win. We went, and we lived or died. Most of us did live, but too many of us died believing in some higher truth that was not being reflected in our presence there. With that in mind, I want to share one more "incident" from my life in Vietnam.

At some point after I was transferred to the 173rd, I volunteered to go through Jungle Warfare Training at a military base located in An Khe in the Central Highlands. It was my privilege, at that time, to be the first person in our unit to ever do this. Upon arriving in An Khe, I began intense training, which included weapons usage, recognition of and avoidance of booby traps, setting up ambush formations, enemy tunnel exploration, rapidly applied first aid techniques, and whatever else seemed to be of importance for surviving in hostile situations. The instructions provided during the training were carried out by experienced infantry combat veterans. It was very thorough and intense, and our training regimen ended with a helicopter assault exercise, with a drop-off point several miles outside of An Khe, in the mountains. On the day of the assault, we did not expect to have contact with enemy forces (this was an exercise), but we were well-equipped if contact did occur (we were in an active war zone).

Early in the morning of the exercise, we loaded into Huey helicopters and were transported into a mountainous, heavily jungled area. After an uneventful drop-off, we formed up and set out on patrol. I was on point, moving out in front of the other men, slowly and methodically surveying the thick vegetation around me, watching the ground beneath and in front of me for any trip wires or booby traps. After several minutes of moving forward (I have no recollection of how much time had actually transpired), I stopped, raised my fist in the air to stop those behind me, and then turned to see that everyone was alright. But to my astonishment, there was no one behind me. I froze in place. Where the hell was everybody? I couldn't yell out to them without giving my position away to Charlie. I certainly couldn't fire my M-16. So, I dropped into a crouch and tried to process what was happening. I did not panic, but I was not even close to being relaxed. And as I squatted there, I suddenly became aware of the thunking, revolving helicopter blade noise high above me. Looking up, I saw four Hueys, loaded with soldiers, flying away from my location. I realized in that instant that

I was being left alone in a heavily jungled area, in rough terrain that I knew nothing about, several miles away from the base camp in An Khe. I was by myself in enemy territory.

What I also knew, in a general sense, was which direction I would need to go in order to somehow return to the military base on foot, if I chose to attempt it. My first decision revolved around determining whether I should stay in place and wait for a rescue team or set out and make my way back toward base camp while trying to avoid anything that even remotely looked like a trail. My mind told me that since they had left without me, there could have been a report of an enemy sighting in the area, and the patrol was called off. The problem was: why didn't they let me know?

Without further hesitation, I concluded that staying in place was not a good idea, so I started walking, while worrying about NVA or Viet Cong who might be moving in the same area. It was early morning, and I moved at a slow, steady pace, carefully watching every step I took. Even though I was avoiding trails, I was worried about trip wires, punji stake pits, and Bouncing Betties (nothing I wanted to have contact with). After a period of time had elapsed in complete silence, I became aware of Vietnamese voices conversing, and I immediately moved into heavier foliage to avoid any possible contact. It could have been friendly villagers from the area having a conversation, but I was not going to risk finding out.

The dense jungle foliage created a high level of awareness inside myself, as I was fearful of snakes—pit vipers, to be exact. We had a saying about vipers back then:

"One step and you're dead, Fred." Those words were good enough for me. Also, the heavier vegetation was slowly transitioning into areas of thick Elephant Grass. Elephant Grass (I'm not sure why they call it that) can grow as high as eight feet tall, and it spreads out to cover a lot of ground. The blades of the grass are very sharp—razor sharp—and my choice was to either move through it or retrace my steps and go down a well-worn trail (if I could find one). Elephant Grass became my choice, and as I moved through it, it tore small rips into my jungle fatigues and cut the skin on my legs, hands, and face—anywhere where I made contact with it. The cuts were very much like the stinging abrasions made when a person accidentally scratches themselves while shaving; nothing deep or life-threatening, but sufficient enough to let me know they were there. I was hurting like all hell due to heavy sweat irritating my raw skin. It seemed like I was in that stuff for hours, but eventually, it thinned out, giving way to friendlier terrain and kinder plant growth. Despite the pain and doubt I was experiencing, I continued to believe I had made the right choice in my direction and chosen route.

I walked on for what felt like endless miles on that day, right through the stifling heat of the afternoon and a brief rain shower, toward the gradually setting sun. And, several hours later, as the terrain continued to thin out and become more conducive to movement, I was finally able to see Basecamp An Khe in the reachable distance. Early that evening, just as complete darkness closed in, I walked into the Jungle School Headquarters building and let them know I was back.

A couple of officers and enlisted men were there when I appeared, like a ghost, from nowhere. I looked like shit: my skin was scratched all to hell, my fatigues were in shreds, I was tired, and I was wondering out loud why in the hell I had been left in the mountains. After recovering from their own shock and surprise in seeing me standing before them, they quickly explained that the men who were behind me on patrol had somehow lost sight of me, realized that we had somehow become separated, and thought I had been captured. Since they couldn't find me, they lifted off, sent word of my capture (or MIA) to my home unit, and started the paperwork related to my disappearance.

Now, standing before them, I was heartily complimented on my ability to work my way back into An Khe and the base. I was provided with a new set of fatigues, had a good shower, was checked over by a medic, ate a good meal, and had a good night's sleep. My unit was notified of my return, and paperwork related to my disappearance was discontinued. Early the next day, I hopped a helicopter ride back to my home unit. I had successfully passed the Jungle School course, and my unit welcomed me back as a hero (although I didn't see anything heroic about what I had done). What stuck in my mind, though, was the always reiterated message: "We leave no one behind."

As I have stated earlier, I was not a combat infantryman. There were times in Vietnam when I wished I had gone in that direction, but such was not to be my fate. Fate is a bothersome word to me; it is always spoken of in hindsight. During my tours in Vietnam, I witnessed and experienced many things, both joyful and horrible. I grew to love and hate the country at times, but I loved the people of South Vietnam and found them to be caring and appreciative of America's presence there. Over the ensuing years, following my return home, any animosity I felt toward the North Vietnamese military dwindled, and I have never harbored any negative feelings toward them. My belief is that we had no reason to be in confrontation with them in the first place.

While serving in Vietnam, I traveled alone at times, and sometimes with others. I walked through thick jungle, endless rice paddies, and small, isolated villages and towns in the Central Highlands and along the coast. A part of me still loves the immense beauty of the country and the people who live there. Regardless of my experiences there, I have no regrets about choosing to go. I can also say that, despite coming back to America in one piece, I discovered, when I took that final flight home, that I had left a part of myself behind—a part of me which will remain there forever. Over the course of the next few years, I married, started college, developed PTSD, and had hearing problems due to both my tympanic membranes being seriously damaged (I am completely deaf in my right ear). I was suffering from Survival Guilt (a story not to be told here), and my soul was deeply shaken.

Without really realizing it, I brought to Gloria my unwanted baggage from Vietnam. She loved me, and I loved her, and as our years together came and went, we worked through many issues related to my past. Now that she has left this earth, I find that my soul has, once again, been shaken to its very core, but in ways I have never before experienced.

Gloria's death, for me, is much deeper than anything I had ever encountered during Vietnam, or in my childhood, and I am now painfully aware that she is not here to love me out of losing her. Or perhaps she is here, and I have just been unable to see that fact.

***

After we married, it became my habit to routinely engage in daily exercise. I loved to run (which was a carryover from my high school years), and later, I graduated into road race bicycling. After work and on weekends, I would literally run anywhere from five to fifteen miles each day, keeping myself in excellent physical condition. Gloria, who was not an exerciser, would worry about me during such jaunts but eventually accepted this behavior, although she thought it was extreme. What I never realized about my running was that it was an effective way for me to calm myself. I just enjoyed it without ever processing the fact that I needed it, especially as my problems with PTSD became more pronounced. I finally gained insights into how effective exercising really was after an episode where I became frustrated and angry one day and took off for what turned out to be a twenty-mile bicycle ride. During that ride, I found that all the tension and irritation I had been experiencing were completely dissipated. I was relaxed and calm. From that time on, running and bicycling became my default mode for decompressing when stressed out. Exercise helped me think and process any anxiety or anger I was feeling. Even better was the fact that running and bicycling are not generally considered team sports and don't involve interpersonal interactions. I could run and ride by myself and be perfectly happy. Besides, I rarely met anyone who was crazy enough to "get into going" with me for a jaunt. My exercise became both a favorite activity and, when necessary, a form of healing for me—especially in relation to PTSD.

Post-Traumatic Stress Disorder (PTSD) slowly began to surface in my day-to-day life after my return home from Vietnam. Technically, from a psychological point of view, when we first married, there was no such thing as PTSD. We joined hands in 1969, and PTSD (as a formal diagnosis) would not be recognized until about 1980. Because PTSD did not formally exist, it was not something being addressed or treated in relation to a veteran's ability to return to "normal" civilian life. Veterans came home and simply went back to living—NOT.

Certainly, I had selected a positive "treatment" for myself involving physical exercise. I was very active and very healthy. Running and biking served to raise my heart rate, strengthen my body, and allowed me to think through my problems without taking them out on those around me, especially those with whom I had regular, ongoing contact (like my wife, for instance). Through exercising, I learned some very positive lessons about keeping myself active and directed when confronting difficulty. And whatever my physical focus was on, my mental focus was always in coordination with it, searching for a solution to whatever I was being presented with—this included flashbacks and bad memories of my experiences in Vietnam. I learned that simple things in life can be very helpful when the world is turning upside down.

***

More and more, during the time that Gloria and I were actively trying to process her cancer diagnosis, I struggled within myself about how to release my stress and ever-present anxiety in a positive way. Anger had never been a serious issue for me; resolving issues through processing was more my style. Gloria's illness and eventual death, however, left me in a situation where I was "up shit creek, without a paddle." I couldn't use humor, and I had no safe outlets (at least in my mind) to release the hurt and pain I was feeling. Over time, after losing her and finding no relief from the pain, I chose to participate in a structured grief-group situation—a decision that turned out to be a lifesaver for me.

One of the first questions to be explored by our group was, "Were we angry at God for our loved one's death?" I was perplexed by that question. My response was that I do not believe in a God who kills or punishes people. For me, there is life, and there is death; they are two sides of the same coin. We are human, and for better or worse, we understand that with our birth also comes our inevitable death. I think that response represented the beginning of a long and arduous journey toward healing for me—one I have yet to complete, and I fear I very likely never will.

Our moment on this planet is to live and to love. We must survive, and we recognize that everyone else must do the same. I could be angry. I could blame God. And, at the most convenient level, I could blame my neighbors (doctors for failing to heal, for instance) for all the negative things that have happened in my life, in Gloria's life, and in the world in general. But blaming serves no purpose; it is a curse rather than a cure. I suppose that anger, in some situations, might serve to jump-start our innate survival mechanisms, but we must be careful. Gloria died due to the presence of cancer on and in her liver. She and I were very aware of the confusion and disruption racing through our minds when we were told about what was happening in her body. We had to repeatedly remind each other to try to relax, take deep breaths, and try to redirect our thinking. The only thing needing to be added to that formula was to become busy and move. Taking long walks or getting involved in "projects" helped us calm and quiet our overactive minds. Going deeper into our individual relationships with God often helped quiet our confusion and fear. I once said to her, "Hell, I'm a doctor of the human mind. I have spent my entire adult life engaged with people struggling to survive, and yet I'm not able to help myself, or you." She just laughed, smiled at me, and said, "Yeah. But you're not a real doctor." Of course, she was right. I am not a "real" doctor. Still, to this very day, I don't blame God, and I don't blame doctors. Life is death, and death is life.

***

When Gloria was first diagnosed with a terminal illness, we found that we still had "time" to live and experience life as fully as we could. But as the years went flying by, we began to realize that a clock was ticking, over which we had no control. Gradually, as she grew weaker, I began a process of withdrawing from what I considered to be a normal life. Running, bicycling, golfing (not really a sport to me), and other activities that I enjoyed, became part of my past. Keeping her safe, comfortable, and loved became my only focus. I tried to give the appearance that I was strong, but in fact, I was collapsing inside myself. She knew this, but there was nothing she could do about it. Life was taking its course, and whatever control we tried to manifest to ourselves or others was nothing more than an illusion—like a house of cards. For the most part, I was with her twenty-four hours a day, every day, during the last two years of her life. Our daughters came, bringing our grandchildren, and we basked in their presence. Gloria was fiercely devoted to our family, especially our grandchildren, who were all taller than she was at the time of her death.

***

During the last six months of Gloria's life, we also engaged with hospice. Hospice visited on a routine basis to take her pulse, check her blood pressure, and provide her with medication to stave off the painful impact of lesions increasingly surfacing on her liver. Nurses came, assessed her situation, discussed her fears with her, and then moved on to other patients. They were always straightforward with both of us about the symptoms and expected progression of her disease, and they spoke of their amazement about her "bravery" as she moved forward through what she was experiencing. They were surprised, right to the very end, that neither of us panicked or backed away from what loomed ahead of us (although I was presenting a totally false impression). And unexpectedly for me, on the morning Gloria died, the hospice nurse who arrived to check her lifeless body and provide a time of death broke down and cried with my daughters and me as Gloria's body was placed in an ambulance and whisked away from us, forever. In retrospect, I am now beginning to realize that everything I thought I might have known—relating to my childhood and my experiences in Vietnam—was part of a series of profound lessons that would bring me to this point in my life. And I will say that I do not believe in hindsight—it's too convenient. None of us can predict the future.

Chapter Ten

A Marriage Made in Heaven

A successful marriage requires falling in love many times, always with the same person.

Mignon McLaughlin

Our marriage ceremony, and the reception following it, was one of the all-time greatest experiences of my young life. I was twenty years old, and Gloria was twenty-one. She was my elder by ten months, and that fact was destined to become the subject of some great humor over the years when I would accuse her of being a cradle robber. I met Gloria while I was on R&R (Rest and Relaxation) after completing my second tour of duty in Vietnam. The manner in which we met has always been a wonderful story, and I love to share it with anyone willing to listen. It goes like this:

While in Vietnam, I started receiving letters through the USO from a girl living in Corpus Christi, Texas. We wrote back and forth for several months, and when I told her that I was coming up for R&R (a term she probably didn't understand until I explained it to her), she invited me to visit with her in Corpus Christi. That was an offer I couldn't refuse. It goes without saying, but I'll say it anyhow, that I had sex on my mind. I accepted her invitation, and we made plans for her to pick me up at the Corpus Christi airport. The plan was that I would stay with her in her home for several days while we were "getting to know each other." Well, that day finally arrived, and as I stepped off the plane in Corpus Christi, I quickly scanned the awaiting visitors, and there she was. We locked eyes immediately. And as I moved toward her, I realized that she was standing next to another girl, somewhat younger, who I thought might be a friend or a sister to her. She approached me, introduced herself and her friend, and I instantly became aware of the fact that the girl with whom I had locked eyes just moments before was not the girl I had agreed to meet at the airport. The girl I was meeting, standing next to the girl I had locked eyes with, as fate would have it, was sixteen years old, did not have a driver's license, was in high school, and (of course) still living with her parents.

She was my pen pal, but she failed to mention any of this in our correspondence. The girl standing next to her, the one with the beautiful eyes, was a friend who lived down the street from my pen pal and was going to college. Pen pal's friend had agreed to drive her to the airport to pick me up. To complicate matters, my pen pal had somehow convinced her parents to allow me to stay at their home. So, basically, I was going (unknowingly) to visit some kid who was still in high school and had misrepresented herself in our exchange of letters. As I waded through this conundrum during the drive into Corpus, I found that her friend, the one with the beautiful eyes, was a pleasant, very easy person to talk with. In fact, she was the only one talking, because my pen pal seemed to be speechless, exhibiting a total loss for words.

As we drove along, the girl with the beautiful eyes and I discussed my upcoming strange arrangements, and she—her name was Gloria—dropped me and my pen pal at my pen pal's home. I have to refer to her as "pen pal" because I have no recollection of her name. I will say that her parents were very nice, very welcoming, and very appropriately protective of their daughter; and I wondered what could have possessed them to allow their child to meet with me in this manner.

My first (and only) night in their home, following introductions and general bantering, was spent sleeping in a room with two twin beds in it. I occupied one bed, and my pen pal's father occupied the other. He snored like a freight train all night long (almost worse than a late-night mortar attack). It was very awkward, very disturbing, in at least a million different ways. The next morning, after a delicious breakfast made by my pen pal's mother, I received a call from my pen pal's friend, Gloria, who lived a couple of streets away with her family.

Gloria asked me how things were going, and I responded, in detail, about my night. She then explained to me that she had informed her father about my situation. Her father, a World War II Navy veteran, had compassion for veterans serving in Vietnam. After hearing "the story," he decided to pay for my stay for the next two nights at a hotel in downtown Corpus, on Ocean Drive. He also gave permission for Gloria to pick me up in her car each morning and show me around the city. I don't think he necessarily trusted me as much as he had total confidence and faith in Gloria to do the right thing. Following that conversation, I humbly thanked my pen pal and her parents for allowing me the comfort of staying in their home, explained to them the awkwardness (for me) of the situation, and then waited for Gloria to pick me up and whisk me away. And whisk me away, she did.

Gloria and I spent the second day of my, to be brief, visit with no further contact with my pen pal. Again, I want to emphasize that in my referring to that young girl as "pen pal," I am doing so with no disrespect. She was a very nice, very naive person, and her parents were gracious and accepting of me. It still amazes me, to this day, that they allowed a complete stranger to enter into their home to visit with their young daughter without knowing anything about who I was as a person.

Gloria, on our first day together, gave me a grand tour of the city she had grown up in. We ate at various locations, and she drove me along Ocean Drive, which paralleled the bay, looking out at the calm, quiet ocean that stretched to the distant horizon. We talked about music and food, books and movies, and whatever else came to mind. We strolled along the T-Head and L-Heads, and it seemed as if we had known each other our entire lives. She explained to me that she was attending college at Texas A&I in Kingsville (later to become Texas A&M, Kingsville), studying to become an elementary school teacher. I explained that college was also a goal for me, but I wasn't certain about what my major might be. Later that afternoon, after spending a wonderful time just being with each other, she dropped me back at the hotel, and she drove home. As evening settled in, I called her, wanting (needing) to hear the softness of her voice. She questioned me about what I'd been doing since she dropped me off, wondering if I had done any further exploring. I laughed, explaining to her that, as a matter of fact, I had just met the girl whom I would marry and spend the rest of my life with. There was a silent pause. She inquired as to who that might be. I replied, "Why, you, of course." We became quiet, both lost in our individual thoughts, then laughed with one another and talked for an endless period of time about nothing in particular. Our talking seemed to be as natural as breathing, and finally, as the evening became night, she reluctantly brought our conversation to a close, telling me she would pick me up in the morning.

The next day (day three), she arrived at the hotel, and we decided to walk along Ocean Drive and, again, visit the T-Head and L-Head, where vendors sold shrimp, crab, and a host of other ocean-related fare. Gloria, with her beautiful eyes, was dressed in clothing appropriate for a tropical climate—casual and light. I, on the other hand, having no "civilian clothing," was wearing my dress greens and boots. As we were crossing Ocean Drive to approach the bay side, I stopped in the middle of the street, dropped to one knee, took her hand in mine, and proposed to her. "Will you marry me?" I asked. And without any hesitation, she smiled that soft smile of hers, laughed joyfully, and said, "I will."

It is important for you to understand that Gloria was raised in a traditional Mexican-American family. I was aware that I would need to ask her mother and father for permission to marry their daughter. However, this was day three, and Gloria was going to drive me back to the airport so I could fly to San Diego, California, to spend a day with my biological mother and my sisters and brothers, and then go on to Oakland, California, to catch a flight back to Vietnam. I expressed my concern to her about my need to talk with her parents. She assured me that she would talk to them and they would understand my circumstances—she would make them understand. I also discussed with her the fact that I had no engagement ring to present to her, but as soon as I got to San Diego, I would go to a jewelry store, pick one out, and mail it to her overnight. She was completely understanding and said she would be watching and waiting for it.

Later that same day, as I was in the air heading to San Diego, Gloria was conversing with her parents about my proposal for marriage and her acceptance of it. She later explained to me that both her parents had immediate concerns about what was happening in our sudden relationship. Her dad expressed his worry that our quick commitment to one another was just a fling based on my loneliness, due to being overseas involved in a war. He suggested that she be cautious and not expect a ring or, for that matter, even any further communication from me. She, in turn, assured him that such would not be the case. And, two days later, as if to prove her point, while I was flying back to Vietnam, she received her engagement ring. She slipped it on her finger and showed it to her parents. Her father, with a look of appreciation and surprise in his eyes, said, "Well, I'll be damned." That was fifty-seven years ago. I finished my third tour of duty, came back to the United States, and we married (which I will now talk about in detail). We were happily married and intensely in love for fifty-three years.

Even now, since she has passed, she is with me. She was my joy then, and she remains my joy now. I loved her when she was living, and I love her still, even in death. Joy and grief always come together—just as do life and death. I didn't understand that when we first married, but I understand it now. I am still in awe! Three days. We didn't really know each other; we simply trusted and allowed life to take its course. Amazing beyond words, and our love grew deep.

***

Having returned to my unit in Vietnam, I wrote a long letter to Gloria's parents and formally requested permission to marry their daughter. She later related to me, in one of her letters, that they both were very impressed with my attention to their beliefs, and they told me that my request was fully granted with all their blessings. I completed my third and final tour of duty and returned to the United States and our wedding ceremony. And, in accordance with tradition, prior to our actual wedding, Gloria and I were always "supervised" when together: we had a constant escort. Supervisory duties were assigned to be carried out by her youngest brother (nine years old at the time), whose continuous presence in our midst ensured that there would be no "hanky-panky" during our interactions. Of course, the meaning of the words "hanky-panky" was oblivious to our young guide; he was just hanging out, having fun with us. We married in Corpus Christi, Texas, on May 2nd, 1969.

***

As a brief aside, Gloria's mother was more "traditional" in certain areas of life and behavior than her father. Humorously, at least for Gloria and me, on one occasion shortly after we became married and were still living in her parent's home, we decided to take a shower together. Her mother became apoplectic, and immediately after we dressed, proceeded to read us the riot act, informing us that bathing together in her house was disrespectful to both her and Gloria's father. We listened with a bewildered sense of wonder, mildly protested (mostly carried out by Gloria), and avoided taking showers together in her parent's home. Her father was not aware of that conversation taking place, and in our opinion, it was doubtful that he would have had any concerns about our bathing habits. Oh well, back to our wedding.

***

Having literally just returned from Vietnam, and not yet settled into "civilized" society, I was experiencing a few mild adjustment concerns. In Vietnam, I was used to drinking a few beers with my buddies, sleeping in a tent or on the ground, and cussing a lot. Cussing in a war zone is as natural as breathing and is generally not done in anger: it is more like a second language, and engaged in normally with a great deal of humor at times. As could be expected, war seems to bring out a wide variety of "inappropriate" expressions in one's day-to-day vocabulary. So, I was having to be very conscious of any possible socially undesirable behaviors on my part in terms of my use of language when interacting with others. In other words, I had to pay close attention to my well-developed habit of cussing.

It was just a natural part of verbal exchanges in Vietnam, and I must say that I had become quite fluent. Surprisingly, I actually handled myself pretty well—for the most part.

Our wedding reception was a fantastic night of dancing, picture-taking, laughing, and enjoying the company of four hundred and some people, of whom three hundred and ninety-five were friends and relatives of Gloria, and five were from my biological family (one of those, my best man, being my mother's seventh (?) husband, whom I had never met). I was completely overwhelmed and became totally engrossed in the amazing amount of food (it wasn't C-rations or basecamp mess hall dishes) being offered at our reception. Even better than the food was the music and dancing. Gloria's father had hired a local band, and she and I danced, and danced, and danced. Neither of us wanted to stop dancing; we were having such a wonderful, fantastic time. The entire wedding ceremony and the reception that followed were so fucking great. I said that in front of several of the wedding guests. WHOOPS. It was even better than sitting at the dining room table and politely asking someone to "please pass me the fucking butter." WHOOPS. And, strangely, as the evening wore on, several of the wedding guests began giving us hints and direct suggestions that we needed to leave the party and go to the hotel where we had reservations for the night. Some, politely, stated that we needed to consummate our marriage. WHOOPS. No one could believe we had stayed at the reception for as long as we did (probably my fault); but we were having the time of our lives. Eventually, an unruly group of wedding guests formed a mob, and they, more or less, shoved us out the door of the reception hall. We were happy they did. WHOOPS.

Two days later, we hopped into our "new" car, a Ford Comet, owned by Gloria's dad, which we paid him a few hundred dollars for (if I remember correctly), and we set off on our honeymoon trip—traveling through West Texas, along the U.S./Mexico border, heading for the West Coast. Once in California, we ventured as far north as San Francisco and the Golden Gate Bridge. This was to be Gloria's first adventure outside the state of Texas (other than a trip to California at an earlier age with her family to visit relatives, and a few jaunts across the border into Mexico). It goes without saying that over the next fifty years or so, Gloria and I would become seasoned world travelers, and she would love every minute of the traveling she did.

One incident, that turned out to be hilarious, occurred shortly after we began our honeymoon as we were driving north along the border. We had a flat tire (not funny), and we were, literally, in the middle of nowhere in the desert. Of course, being the hero and big-shot war veteran that I was, I assured her that all would be corrected forthwith. I hopped out of the car, popped the trunk, and retrieved the jack and the spare, ready to change that tire. So far, I was "THE MAN." I removed the flat tire without difficulty, but as I started to mount the spare, to my confusion and dismay, it didn't fit on the awaiting rim. I shifted and rotated it, clockwise and counterclockwise, without success. And as I became more and more frustrated and perplexed, thinking the wrong spare had been placed in the trunk, I looked up and saw that Gloria was laughing. "What are you laughing about?" I inquired. She looked at me, with a glint in her eye, and said, "Why don't you just turn the tire around?" With a sheepish look on my face, I looked down at the tire, paused thoughtfully, and burst out in hysterical laughter right along with her. So much for being the hero. I then successfully mounted the spare, and our trip continued.

It was on our honeymoon trip that I introduced Gloria to my love of singing. In high school, I had had a pretty good voice, and I sang in the choir for a couple of years. The very first song I ever sang to her, as we journeyed westward, was "The Shadow of Your Smile," as sung by Johnny Mathis. She had never heard it before. It was one of my favorite love songs. I won't write the words of the song here (and I did change a few words here and there when singing it), but I think the reader would find the lyrics special. I would sing this song to her again and again, over the years of our marriage, at her request—as would be the case with many other songs I had learned growing up. Singing to Gloria became a habit that carried through our entire marriage (with dancing not far behind).

Now, as I think back to the words of that first song, I find myself wondering if there wasn't some hidden prophecy in them—a prophecy too deep for either of us to really make contact with or process. It seems, at least to me, that there was a message lying in wait in those words, which would, over the years, slowly reveal itself. Of course, such thoughts have come as hindsight, and hindsight, as I stated earlier, while seeming to be valid, is nothing more (in my opinion) than reinterpretations of events we have undergone in our past, without being able to project them into our future until it is done. And yet…

***

Since Gloria's death, I have developed a habit of waking from sleep at about 6:30 to 7:00 A.M. I generally roll over onto my back, cross my hands and arms over my chest, and let my mind gradually come in contact with whatever the new day might bring. I monitor the feelings in my body and focus on what my emotions are. Often, I experience a mild feeling of dread over the idea of crawling back into the world of conscious existence again. With no exception, I am aware of the fact that she is not here with me. I am alone with my thoughts, and my ever-present sadness, over not being able to reach out and touch her. I can hear the steady breathing of my dog Luke, lying in his bed, waiting for me to rise up and start another day.

The house is dead silent (pun intended). I think, at times, it is like a mortuary—for lack of a more apt description. I sense that things are becoming "better," but I am not yet sure what that means. I become aware of the ticking of the nightstand clock. Gradually, I allow sounds from outside to gain awareness in my mind: the buzz of a chainsaw, a car or a truck driving by, trash being collected, dogs barking. Before Gloria's death, I had always enjoyed the quiet birth of new days. Our house has always been, and still is (I think), a place of comfort, peace, and serenity—a place where people can relax and feel calm. But now, at times, the same quietness moves through me as though an ominous force is pressing down on me. I think about turning on the television, to break the emptiness, but quickly dismiss such thoughts. Television, luckily for me, early in the morning, is the equivalent of drinking a beer or having a mixed drink to start the day. My episodes of physically painful grief are fewer now, in comparison with when she first died, but when they do occur, they continue to be overwhelming. I know, regardless of who I'm with or what I'm doing, I'm going to have to walk this walk by myself. This time in my life is the true meaning of entering into the desert alone, and searching for my strength to face life again. I think of Jesus asking that the cup be passed on, realizing that it cannot be, and then rising up and completing the life he was meant to live. Each and every one of us, without question, will have our moments in the desert. I wonder when I will feel the strength, once again, to go on living without looking back—maybe never. I sense that the act of remembering may very well be my salvation.

***

From the first time we met, until this very moment, Gloria and I have been together—first in life and now in death. During our marriage, she was the literal "light" of my life. We loved each other with an intensity beyond my capacity to adequately describe. I was a Vietnam Veteran. Little did either of us know what lay ahead of us as we began our journey as husband and wife. And little did either of us realize that a part of my being had been damaged irreparably from my experiences in a war that followed me home. The ugly, unwanted specter of PTSD would soon begin to assert itself in both our lives, and facing its presence would become the first of many challenges we would grapple with and overcome.

Chapter Eleven
Note on Learning to Live with One Another

A perfect Marriage is just two imperfect people who won't give up on each other.

Kate Stewart

Marriage in America, over the past several decades, has involved a massive change in philosophical foundations. At one time, the consensus attitude about coming together in matrimony was focused on the idea that once two became one, the relationship was to be permanent, barring only death. There is much of value in that type of orientation. Whether it is realistic or not, however, is questionable. Marriage, like all things in life, has evolved, and it now makes complete sense to seriously consider divorce in the presence of sexual, physical, or mental abuse, which seem to be common issues in many relationships. Unfortunately, however, the pendulum has swung to a point where "married today, and divorced tomorrow" has become a prevalent attitude in our society. And, disturbingly, issues of various forms of simple disagreements and personal differences have resulted in one or the other partner, under such circumstances, rationalizing their way out of relationships, declaring them to be beyond repair. The real focus of any marriage should be directed toward learning to live with one another, while realizing that doing so is an ongoing process requiring hard work, dedication, and devotion. Having an open mind is a necessary element of any marriage. Where two people meet, there will be disagreements and problematic situations, which must be addressed and resolved. A good marriage is an exercise in learning to communicate and, ultimately, in finding a middle ground where relationships can be mutually satisfying, without having to be perfect or self-compromising. Whether you choose to squeeze the toothpaste tube in the middle or the end is not grounds for a divorce. Your marriage, if you can dare to see it that way, is an adventure. It is also hard work.

I am (so I have been told) one of the easiest people on earth to get along with (I seriously doubt that Gloria would have agreed with that). I will listen, for lengthy periods of time, to others rant and rave about why their lives are so miserable, unfulfilling, and lacking in meaningful relationships. I have a clear understanding that people, in general, are afraid, sad, and fearful about life, and they oftentimes become overwhelmed to the point of not being able to cope with what they are presented with. I, too, have found myself, in the last few years, in the same position on many occasions. What is most disturbing, though, is that many people, when confronted with traumatic events, will give up the will or desire to live. They will, depending upon the degree of threat they are experiencing, consciously back away from their instinct to survive (or so it seems). As a therapist, I have always felt more positive about potential outcomes when confronted with angry, acting-out individuals, as opposed to individuals reflecting issues of depression and loss of life energy. Following my experiences in Vietnam, I devoted my life to attempting to help others, either directly or indirectly, to learn to stand up for themselves, believe in themselves, and reach for their dreams, believing that, despite all the barriers they face, their dreams are attainable. Angry people, at least outwardly, appear to move in a life-affirming direction, while depressed, hopeless people appear to stop moving at all. Gloria's death put my belief system, and my ability to survive, to the ultimate test. It is not that I want to die (I do want to live), but I haven't known how or whether I can. My grief has ultimately, though, led me to a deeper understanding of my own strengths and weaknesses, and grief is becoming one of my greatest teachers.

Gloria, like me, was also an easygoing, caring person, and she was loved and respected by almost everyone who came into contact with her and took the time to get to know her. She was a schoolteacher and a loving soul by nature. She and I did not always agree on how we, or others, should react or respond when faced with stress or hardship, but we always tried to keep an open mind. She was rarely confrontational (except with me) in her interactions, and she avoided arguments as though they were an infectious disease. She did not like to discuss politics, and she veered away from any dialogues about specific religious views or beliefs. Her avoidance of such topics did not include me, however. We had made a pact that we could "agree to disagree." She openly admitted to me that disagreements (stating one's values and personal opinions openly and aggressively) were a source of fear for her. I agreed with her that conflicts and sour feelings could have detrimental effects on interpersonal relationships, but I disagreed with her about avoiding serious issues when they presented themselves. The old saying, "We should let sleeping dogs lie," is surely a guaranteed formula for being severely bitten. I shared with her that thoughts and feelings should be directly addressed without hidden agendas (which always serve as a form of subtle attack from others with whom we disagree). In fact, there were many times during our marriage when I would indicate to her that we should have a good, old-fashioned, hearty disagreement because we were getting along too well; and in my opinion, that was not a good sign. She would, initially, approach such statements very seriously, rejecting them as "not making much sense." But later, as we learned to trust one another, she would laugh right along with me about my ridiculous suggestions, feeling a sense of relaxation in having released built-up negative tension.

Problem resolution became a source of contention between Gloria and me as we learned to live with and interact with one another. While I physically learned to "let off steam" when upset, she, on the other hand, when confronted with trauma or difficulties, had an entirely different approach. Instead of becoming active, she tended to withdraw and become silent. I could always tell when she was upset with me because she became non-communicative. She would refuse to speak, and at times, depending on the depth of her feelings, she would actually retire to our bedroom, lay down, and attempt to drift off to sleep (which she could never do). When we first married, her reaction to an argument would be to verbally express to me her feeling of hurt and upset, and then she would cry and head straight to the bedroom, close the door, and lay on the bed in the dark.

I, of course, saw this as being unhealthy. I later discovered that her mother would do exactly the same thing when arguing with her grown children, or with Gloria's dad. At any rate, when Gloria would isolate herself, I would bug her endlessly and disrupt her self-imposed quiet time (sullen time, as I saw it). I would facetiously accept full responsibility for being the perpetrator of her "bad" feelings, apologize, tell her jokes, and change the subject when she would try to address "the real problem." The real problem was usually not as serious as either of us was making it out to be. I would apologize over and over (even when I felt the "real problem" was not my fault), tell her how sorry I was for my transgression, and literally beg her for forgiveness. She would argue with me about how the "issue" being addressed was not that easy to resolve. I would disagree, continue to apologize again and again, ask for her forgiveness, and before you know it, she would be laughing, holding my hands, and we would be kissing and making out. You get the idea.

Our first five years of life together revolved around my beginning the process of finding employment and enrolling in college. College, in and of itself, was a daunting undertaking. Gloria had completed her Teacher's Degree with financial assistance from her parents (when she first started classes) and later through income from occasional part-time jobs as we struggled to make ends meet. Fortunately, she was able to find a teaching position almost immediately after graduating. I, on the other hand, was seeking out various odd jobs while starting college classes leading to a Ph.D. in Child and Family Counseling. Veterans' Benefits were helpful for my first four years, but beyond that point, we were on our own. We started married life dirt poor, but we were happy. After moving through a series of "nowhere" temporary jobs, I finally landed a direct-care position, working in a state institution for the mentally retarded (a term not used in this day). Along with working and going to school, I was becoming more and more aware of the onset of PTSD in our daily life. It began slowly and seemed to correlate with my frustrations over money and being overwhelmed by college demands, paired with a lack of sleep. I worked and I studied.

At times, when demands seemed unbearable, I would unexpectedly fly into rage. The rages, in turn, seemed to convert into problems with my sleeping patterns, and I would experience horrible nightmares about my time spent in Vietnam. The nightmares, which were very intense, did not necessarily reflect anything that actually happened while I was there, but they were very disturbing. For example, I dreamed on two separate occasions about being killed during firefights with the Viet Cong. As a result, I took to the habit of sleeping with a combat knife under our mattress, and on more than one occasion, in the grips of a nightmare, I would drop from our bed to the floor, knife in hand, and begin crawling out of our bedroom and down the hallway. I was not aware of what I was doing. In my mind, I was crawling through a field in Vietnam. My nightmares woke Gloria and frightened her as she watched me creeping across the floor. She had no idea that I had been mortally wounded and was dying in a firefight. And, even more frightening, during such moments, was when I would jerk upright from sleep, screaming at some invisible nothingness, a black void smothering and swallowing me. As I think back to those frightening times, I become more and more aware of what an amazing person Gloria really was.

Despite her fear, as she watched me moving across the floor and out of the bedroom, she would softly begin to call my name. "Tomas, it's alright. You're here at home. You're right here with me. It's alright." She would never touch me or try in any way to physically redirect me—just a soft voice that gradually found its way into my conscious mind, encouraging me to come back from wherever I had gone. Once fully awake and present, I would spend a great deal of time lying awake processing what was happening inside me. Over time, I finally gave up sleeping with the knife and relegated it to a safe place far from our bedroom. I also contacted the VA, was interviewed by a psychiatrist, and was assigned to a weekly PTSD group with about fifteen other men who were facing similar issues. While the group experience did not totally resolve my PTSD, my night terrors did gradually subside and eventually disappear. Over the years, my PTSD has quieted to a point where loud, unexpected sounds and/or involvement in large groups of noisy people were my only distractions. I had to learn how to control my responses to noisy groups simply because Gloria had a family, including extended members, who could be really animated when everyone got together. In those situations, I learned to disappear. People would say, "Where is Tom?" and begin looking for my hideout. Loud, unexpected sounds, however, still to this day, remain a trigger for a knee-jerk/freeze response, as I process what I am reacting to.

As I learned more effective ways to handle my

problems with PTSD, I suggested to Gloria that she and I should offer, to the wives of veterans, a workshop opportunity focusing on issues surrounding PTSD and the manifestation of its symptoms: specifically, flashbacks and general physical responses to unexpected situations that might arise in ordinary life but are not perceived as ordinary by traumatized veterans. At first, she balked at the idea of talking to large groups (another of her fears) with the spouses of vets. Gradually, though, she agreed to give it a try, and it turned out to be a beneficial experience for not only those attending but for ourselves as well. Over time, we talked to hundreds of wives of vets, and the information was well received and appreciated. Life was moving on, though, and in time we turned our attention to other issues and directions. A final note here is that many marriages involving traumatized veterans have resulted in separations and divorces. Such an outcome was not a consideration for Gloria and me.

Gloria also had her own moments of anxiety as she moved into the world of teaching. Her bad times generally revolved around issues of being annually evaluated for her work in the classroom. While she didn't have nightmares about being assessed, she did, to an extreme degree, experience episodes of fear of failure. In my vernacular, she suffered from low self-esteem, despite being an excellent teacher. For several years, evaluation time would bring stress and tears to her eyes and her otherwise normal life. She hated being "judged" and felt such assessments would reflect some inability on her part. Subsequently, we spent many evenings during those dreaded times talking at length about her actual performance in the classroom and her reasons for downplaying her own abilities. While I won't go into the details of those conversations, I will say that as the years passed, she grew out of her dislike of being evaluated, took it in stride, and became recognized for her ability to work with and provide a high-quality education to her students. She did, in fact, receive numerous awards, including being voted Teacher of the Year (which she was nominated for countless times). She became a supervisor and friend to other teachers, and she was deeply appreciated for her presence in the field of education. She became strong. I hope I was a part of her growth in that process.

Somehow, we survived those first few years of marriage, and the insecurities and problems that came with them. I graduated with a bachelor's degree, found a good job, and then headed back for more school. Eventually, I obtained a double master's degree in psychology and sociology. That improved my options for financial advancement and strengthened my decision to continue on toward a Ph.D. I was, and still am, in many ways a perpetual student of the human mind. Gloria, on the other hand, decided to remain in the classroom setting rather than reaching for higher, more administratively oriented degrees. She absolutely hated school politics, preferring to stay in the trenches. She always told me she was more interested in working with students than in making money. In my mind, she was exactly right.

***

I, in spite of my difficult history before meeting Gloria, have always been a lover at heart. I love the awe and beauty of the world. I loved Gloria and the beauty of her soul and her presence in my life and the life of our children. It has now been nearly two years since her death, and yet here I sit, typing, sometimes crying, remembering the life we had and the fact that she is now gone. I understand that my childhood, with all its disappointments, and my time in Vietnam, where human sorrow and suffering were always present, were the very forces that taught me to stand up and reject the idea that there was nothing left to live for. Gloria was an integral source of life in my return from the dead; she helped me to rekindle the fire, which was still smoldering deep inside. She helped me to continue on with my life, and I, in turn, was able to hold her hand and walk with her into the arms of awaiting death. As I grieve then, and continue to grieve now, I try to go on. It is beyond difficult—especially in the absence of her presence. I cry. I sob. And there have been many times when I have felt that I cannot go on; but go on I will. She and I lived and loved as we moved forward through the Valley of the Shadow. I sincerely hope that you, the reader, might find some comfort in knowing that in your own loss, or losses, your life can, and must, go on. Do not be afraid to shed tears. Do not fear being weak within yourself, or in the view of others. Live and learn from your grief and continue your journey. Know the joy of your humanness and rejoice in your understanding that you are capable of everlasting love.

***

When Gloria died, I (figuratively speaking) found myself prone on the ground, completely devastated. And, lying there, I became aware of being next to a deep, endless abyss, and I could feel my spirit (my soul) begin to separate from my physical body and slowly topple over the edge into a black void. I dropped further and further into the nothingness, which wrapped itself around me, consuming me. I could not feel. I just continued to fall deeper and deeper to a place where there was only darkness and no sound. My body remained far above me and eventually was able to stand, move around, and interact with those attempting to make contact with me. But my spirit (my heart) was broken and lost in that forlorn place. That was the place where I came to know that I would have to be reborn into a world without my love. I began to crawl, to pull myself upward, moving toward a different life. The effort in that place of death has been difficult beyond words, but I have slowly reached a point where I can hear my children calling down to me, crying out, "Daddy, where are you? You need to come back and be with us." I hear and feel their love and their worry, and I call up to them through that terrible emptiness, "I'm almost there, I'm coming. It won't be long." This is what my relationship with grief has been like: alone and wrapped in darkness, even when surrounded by those who love me.

Chapter Twelve

The Hospital Bed

*Your passed loved ones are not dead and gone,
nor are they removed from the life you're still living.
They are with you every single day,
and they aren't missing out on what's happening in your
life, either.*

Rory Walkom

During the month of December 2022, Gloria and I began having discussions about the possibility of having a hospital bed moved into our bedroom, replacing our king bed. It was more my idea than hers. She seemed very leery of sleeping in anything other than her own bed. I explained to her, on more than one occasion, my concerns about the fact that it was becoming more difficult for her to, more or less, climb into our bed. She was short (4' 8"), and our bed was such that she could not just sit back and stretch into it. As her cancer progressed, it had become more and more of a physical challenge for her to crawl into the bed, even with my assistance. I was always ready and willing to help her get into or out of bed, but having a hospital bed (I thought) would be more accessible to her needs. As I relate this story, it comes to my mind that she might have been afraid of the hospital bed, knowing it was another reflection of her one-sided battle with cancer. With reservations, I continued to honor her strength and determination, and backed away from the issue, not wanting to add any more stress to her situation than was already present. She was always strong-minded, and no bed change was made until the day that she dropped onto the carpet, on the way to the bathroom (which was discussed in an earlier chapter). That fall changed everything.

The hospital bed was delivered and set up on 12/30/22. I had gone shopping the day before its arrival and purchased a "nice," colorful bedspread and some attractively designed twin sheets and pillowcases. Celeste's husband and our grandsons came to disassemble our king bed and place it in temporary storage at their home. Gloria was not happy about the change, but she was not in total disagreement with it either. On the evening it was set up and ready for use, I brought a wicker chair for myself into the bedroom and sat it next to where she would sleep. Reading to Gloria was something I had been doing every night, and she always looked forward to it. As I have mentioned before, one of her strongest interests revolved around the experiences of Death Doulas (mediums in contact with the spirits of the dead). Knowing this, I purchased a book written by Debra Diamond, Ph.D., a well-known Death Doula, medium, and author. While I found reading such stories to be somewhat strange from my own personal perspective, Gloria looked forward to them and was able to maintain her attention on their content. I believe our readings gave her hope and a sense of peace.

On the afternoon of the day the hospital bed was set up, as though it had been scripted, both our daughters arrived at our home to visit with us and bring in the New Year. My younger daughter, Heather, is a fanatic for taking pictures and videos of anything and everything involving family. As evening quietly descended upon us, I helped Gloria into her new sleeping arrangement and seated myself next to her to begin our nightly storytelling ritual. She seemed extremely tired, but she actively listened as I began to read. After finishing the first short story, and thinking she had fallen asleep, I paused, sitting in silence, watching her. After a few moments, she opened her eyes, smiled at me, and requested that another story be told. Heather, unbeknownst to me, holding her camera at the ready and standing just on the other side of our bedroom door, pushed the door open and quickly snapped a picture of me sitting in the chair next to the bed, then slowly retreated, quietly closing the door behind her as I began the second story. Once that story was completed, Gloria and I entered into our nightly routine of saying a goodnight prayer—a ritual we had been going through for at least the past year. I would take her hand in mine and say, "If the Lord is willing and the creek don't rise, I'll see you in the morning." She would then repeat those words to me, we would kiss, and I would turn out the light and move into the living room. For some reason, though, on that particular night, I changed the words to the prayer very slightly. As I held her hand, I said, "If the Lord is willing and the creek don't rise, I'll see you in the morning, but if the Lord is not willing, and the creek does rise, you may leave me for now, but know that I will be with you soon." She was having difficulty with the words as she tried to repeat them, and I took her through them two or three times until she was able to say them correctly. She was smiling as I said goodnight to her, and she quickly dropped off to sleep. That was the last night I would ever see her alive.

Later that evening, Celeste entered our room and lay down on the carpeted floor next to the hospital bed. She reached up, took her mother's hand in hers, and fell asleep. Heather had gone to sleep in the bedroom she had grown up in, the one she called her own. I was sleeping in another room. At about 3:00 in the morning, Celeste alerted Heather that their mother was sweating profusely (it was actually body fluid exiting through her pores) and her bedclothes were soaked and needed to be changed. Both girls tenderly bathed her with damp, cool cloths, combed her hair, and talked with her as they made her comfortable. Their mother was responsive and relaxed, and she quickly fell back to sleep again. All was calm until about 6:00 A.M. Celeste, again lying on the floor holding her mother's hand, felt a sudden jerk. Her mother shot upright into an unsteady sitting position and regurgitated a large amount of body fluid mixed with blood onto the bedroom carpet and into a trash can, which Celeste had immediately grabbed and held before her. Celeste yelled for Heather, and Heather ran into the room I was sleeping in and blurted out, "Dad, we need you." I jumped out of bed, put on a pair of jeans and a T-shirt, and rushed to the bedroom. Gloria, my wife, their mother, was dead. Celeste was sitting upright on the edge of the hospital bed with her mother's lifeless body resting against her. I gently reached out and took the place where she was and sat with Gloria's body leaning against my side and shoulder. I sat like that with her for maybe thirty minutes or more. We were, all three of us, in mild shock and completely devastated. Heather, pacing back and forth and using her phone, was able to contact hospice, and hospice began the process of arranging for Gloria to be moved to a mortuary. After closing that call, she then called the people who would be responsible for her cremation and informed them of her mother's death. They, too, began the process of making arrangements.

As I continued to sit with Gloria, I began to notice that her body was losing warmth, and she was becoming cold. I began to quietly cry, and I told the girls I wanted to lie her down and cover her with a blanket to keep her warm. Once that was done, I made sure that her eyes and mouth were closed. She was gone. She was never coming back. The world as I knew it had, in the blink of an eye, ceased to exist. Later that day, after the mortuary had come and taken her away, Celeste and I put a soapy solution into a plastic bucket, dropped down on our knees, and scrubbed the body fluid stains out of the bedroom rug. That soapy solution was mixed as much with our tears as it was with water. Later that same day, my son-in-law and my grandsons, at my request, brought our king bed back and reassembled it, placing it in the exact same position it had been, all those many years she and I had occupied it.

Amazingly, Gloria spent only one night in that unwanted, ugly hospital bed. She had lived a beautiful, adventure-filled, satisfying life, and she left us on her own terms. In this moment, as I sit here writing, I am painfully aware of how much time has gone by since her death, and yet I am STILL at a loss within myself; I miss her so much. I miss her today as much as I did on the day she died. I remain stuck in that dark place, and as I have stated so many times, I wonder if I will ever be truly happy again. I know that my life will go on, but where it will go? I have no idea. I am going through the motions, but I am yet to get somewhere.

***

Gloria was never big on having parties for herself, but she always enjoyed family gatherings, especially those involving her grandchildren. Over the years, following her diagnosis of NASH and with cancer silently making its entrance into her body, she began to slow down and was becoming less and less interested in loud, rambunctious festivities. Too much noise and too many people were beginning to drain her energy. She and I were generally in agreement in our dislike of the "noisy" life and the avoidance of social chaos, but I found myself coming to the conclusion that our 50th Anniversary was an exception to our unwritten rule. As our anniversary approached, she was adamantly against having a celebration, and I, for a change, was adamantly advocating for a family and friends gathering to recognize our accomplishment—fifty years is a long time. We had reached that point where she was resisting and I was persisting, and she was winning. I repeatedly discussed with her the fact that her daughters, her husband, her immediate relatives, her friends, and whoever else was out there, all felt that a 50th anniversary was a special occasion deserving recognition and celebration. Fifty years, although feeling like they flew by in an instant, is not something which will come around a second time. And, in this so-called modern era, two people remaining committed to one another and actually loving each other for that period of time is a rare occurrence; something to be valued and recognized.

One of Gloria's main concerns about hosting a 50th Anniversary party revolved around her medical condition, which involved (among other issues) her bouts of unexpected, unwanted, chronic coughing. At times, the coughing was so intense that a vomiting reflex occurred. If certain foods didn't agree with her, she would often experience intense, unexpected "fits" of coughing, gagging, and then she would rush to the bathroom and throw up. It went without saying that such experiences were embarrassing for her, as well as being exhausting. The coughing, however, was not an everyday occurrence. She did have long stretches between such episodes, and I thought that, under the circumstances, and being careful with her eating choices, she might just get by and enjoy seeing people who loved her and needed contact with her.

As I persisted, though, she insisted that she was just too tired to prepare for a party involving a large group of people. Cooking, setting up tables and chairs, decorating the house—both inside and out—were just too much for her. She felt that the stress of interacting with everyone in attendance would be too difficult, and people would probably find her to be rude and insensitive if she had to withdraw and rest for a while. Mind you, she had cancer of the liver, and all her friends and relatives were aware of that. I had reached a point where I sensed the tables had turned against me, and I would have to relent. Finally, as a last resort, I decided to bring in THE BIG GUNS: enter our daughters, Celeste and Heather. It was a lowdown, dirty play on my part, but I had no choice—and it worked.

Both girls jumped into the controversy immediately

and were very direct in pointing out to their mother that our 50th wedding anniversary would be one of the most important milestones, not only in her life, but also in the lives of everyone in the family. They pointed out that both relatives and friends would love to honor and celebrate the years we had spent together; our relationship was always seen as a miracle in our day and age. And, just as I expected, over a period of endless encouragement from them (nagging, quite frankly), she relinquished and agreed to a gathering of no more than 75 to 80 people—those we were closest to.

Gloria, having reluctantly given in, "supervised" according to how she felt, while the girls, myself, and others did the real work (which had always been a given from the start). The renewal of our vows took place in the backyard of our home and was conducted by one of my best friends, who was the pastor of a church in Waco, Texas. Gloria was very close with his wife, as they had taught together for many years. Delicious home-cooked barbecue was on the menu for the day, and the entire event was paid for by immediate family members. Certainly, it was true, as Gloria said, that putting the celebration together was a difficult task, but her only job, other than worrying, was to sit and watch it come together. I know that, in her mind, in her resistance, she was struggling with her need to be involved, but to all our delight, she was able to accept the situation, and she actually found herself enjoying it.

The people who joined us came from all over Texas (which is no small state to travel across), Georgia, California, and elsewhere. Because of Gloria's overall health needs, we set a specific time for the ceremony to begin and end. We knew she would be totally exhausted by the end of the day, and rest would be first and foremost on her mind. And, just as my daughters and I expected, the gathering turned out to be a blessed day for everyone involved. Without anything being openly said about it, the moments she shared with our visitors were a very simple way for her to say thank you, I love you, and goodbye. I have cherished memories of her loving interactions with one of her female cousins, a lifelong friend who, herself, was terminally ill and would pass away within the following year. They had grown up together and had maintained a close relationship by phone for many years. Her cousin died from complications due to pulmonary fibrosis.

Chapter Thirteen
Panic and Anxiety

<u>Our bodies become lighter, our minds sharper, and our spirits lifted.</u>
<u>When we undergo healing, we are more equipped to help others heal since we are</u>
<u>going through the process. We can speak from places of love and light more fully instead of just places of trauma and despair.</u>

Mayowa Sanusi, 6/13/21

My emotional response to Gloria's initial diagnosis of NASH was a low-keyed feeling of distress. I seemed to go about my daily routines without major problems. However, within just a few weeks, things gradually changed, and I ended up having two major panic attacks within a period of about six months. This was totally uncharacteristic for me because, with one exception involving a caving incident in Kentucky, I had never experienced an actual prolonged panic episode. In that particularly frightening situation, I knew exactly what was happening as I moved through an overwhelming moment of believing I would die. Then, I felt a gradual sense of relief as my awareness that I would live returned to normal. The situation was resolved, and I responded, in-like, by moving on. It was truly disturbing, but its duration was short, and it then seemed to dissolve without further problem other than a permanent memory of what had happened. It was good knowledge to have, but it did not stop me from further caving expeditions.

Unlike my first experience with panic, though, not only were my two attacks frightening, but the symptoms persisted unrelentingly for hours and were accompanied by a fear that I was dying, was depressed and was experiencing feelings of guilt. None of my responses made any sense to me, especially in regards to thinking I might die. When Gloria was informed of her terminal condition, I was fully alive and in good physical health, and my own physical existence was not threatened. To complicate matters even further, I was relating to my panic and fear as signs of personal weakness and incompetence within myself: she was the one diagnosed with a terminal illness, and I was the one internally and outwardly falling apart. And stranger than that, for me, was that she was not experiencing any panic or observable distress at all; she was afraid but managing.

In addition to the psychological issues of depression, guilt, and possible death, my panic attacks (and later anxiety) were also accompanied by a whole series of physical symptoms which included skipping heart beats (palpitations), a chronically upset stomach, high blood pressure, altered blood test values, fatigue, depressed oxygen levels and excruciating amounts of physical pain throughout my body. Is it no wonder that I believed that I was going to die from either a heart attack or outright heart failure? My symptoms, on both occasions of panic, were so pronounced that I actually ended up in a hospital ER. I knew, intellectually, that panic and anxiety are common responses to loss, and suddenly I knew and understood those symptoms on a personal basis.

In the hospital, I was tested, analyzed, and scrutinized from a dozen different points of view: walking the treadmill, blood draws, X-rays, blood pressure monitoring, heart monitoring and other approaches. And, in my case, all the results returned "unremarkable." I had no clearly definable physical medical problems, which would be reflected by the symptoms I was experiencing. My heart was functioning normally, and my health was good. Strangely, though, the medical staff working on my case and reviewing my test findings never once suggested the possibility of "panic" to me. The word panic seemed to be absent from their vocabularies. No matter to me. My training and background told me, without question, that the problem was in my mind, and I was feeling real physical symptoms.

Later, when panic attacks seemed to recede from the picture (which they did), I began to develop ongoing episodes of anxiety, which initially resulted in regular consultations with my general physician, who encouraged me to try any number of different medications to relieve my symptoms. Anxiety, in my case, was of less intensity than panic but of longer duration, almost endless. The physician and I had been good friends for several years, and he was well aware of the fact that I was resistant to the use of medication for anything other than infections or surgical procedures. The fact is that I have a strong resistance to the use of pharmaceuticals of any type. He was also aware that, as a mental health professional, I had serious questions about the use of psychoactive medications for the treatment of difficult behavioral and/or emotional problems. However, with that knowledge in mind, he suggested, for purposes of calming the anxiety I was manifesting, that I try Xanax (it didn't work), Ambien (it didn't work), Melatonin (it didn't work) and several others (none of which served to calm me). Potential side-effects, regardless of effective treatment possibility, turned me off before I was even turned on. So, my approach to the ever-present anxiety I was experiencing was bottom line, to tough it out. I decided to go through my misery rather than chemically altering my own physical body chemistry. It had become my personal perspective that I had seen too many people become addicted to pharmaceuticals without even scratching the surface of what was prompting their problems in the first place. (I need to say here that I am not suggesting that any reader should, in the throes of anxiety, grief, or despair, avoid medications. The use of medications is a personal choice. I made a choice not to use them. What I am saying is, just be careful and proceed with caution when such advice is given).

As I stated previously, the severity of my panic and anxiety was overwhelming. It was so pronounced that, at one brief point, I found myself fearing to leave the confines of my home (was I becoming agoraphobic?). If I engaged in my daily walk with my dog, took the trash out, mowed my yard, or went to the store for groceries (or whatever), I was totally convinced that I would suffer and die from a heart attack. Again, I did not discuss this with her. I still had an active drive to protect her. And, despite all my fears and misgivings, I forced myself to do all those things I was trying to avoid. I repeatedly said to myself that I was being irrational (which there was no doubt about), and hand-in-hand, Gloria and I continued on our journey, becoming, in some vague sense, more aware that we were, and always had been, walking through the Valley of the Shadow.

There were countless times, for instance, when I had to force myself out the front door with my dog, Luke, leaving Gloria by herself, knowing she or I could die during our separation. But, out the door, we went, to hell with the danger. As a humorous aside here (although it's not really all that funny), I actually added a second handhold to the leash I carried so that if I dropped dead on the street during our walk, my dog would be with me until someone found my body. I mowed the grass and took out the trash. I lived, and I knew I was alive, sometimes marveling at that fact. I kept putting one foot in front of the other each and every day. If it sounds silly to you, so be it. It sounds silly to me, but that is what happened. Irrationality, flamed by anxiety and grief, was fueling my behavior. My anticipatory grief (if you will) was fully active, and I was determined to understand it and bring it to rest. I was learning to live while becoming painfully aware that a part of my soul was in the process of dying, and nothing could change that ugly fact. All the counseling and all the real help I had provided to others, or that was provided to me, came crashing down. I had helped thousands and yet was at a loss to help myself or Gloria (not true, but it sure seemed like it). By continuously forcing myself to go beyond my self-imagined limitations and weaknesses, I became, day-by-day, stronger. I am still working on it, but I think I'm getting a peek at what is on the other side of the mountain. And I now realize that this is exactly what I had taught others to do as well. As the old saying goes, "Physician heal thyself." I began to question whether mowing the yard and taking long bicycle rides or walks with my dog might serve to heal me in the same manner in which an antibiotic might resolve a bacterial infection. It came to my mind that the normal daily activities that I, in my grief, tended to withdraw from might be the very agents of healing that could bring me back to life.

Grief and anxiety are closely bound to one-another. The mental symptoms of grief are the natural result of the death of a loved one, paired with the physical symptoms of the anxiety that follows. I felt ashamed and embarrassed. I am a man. I saw myself as having the responsibility of caring for Gloria and protecting her as her cancer progressed. Fortunately, as time moved forward, I began to realize that I might be in error in my interpretation about what I was confronting within myself. I, at first, fought my increasing insights. Still, something deeper was afoot, and I was actively (by not giving in) moving toward a new understanding of panic and anxiety, an understanding that could serve in the process of my own return to something that at least resembled normalcy.

In spite of my problems, I was able to recognize that all my symptoms were, at base, irrational and dangerous for my continued health, and they were also something I felt I could develop control over. Consciously, I realized that I could override most of my symptoms when interacting with others. For me, that was a curious but positive insight. It allowed me to focus on learning how to bring their expressions under my direct control, not an easy endeavor. I could actually pretend to be normal in the presence of family, friends, and others; I could fake it to make it and fall apart later. Besides, who in their right mind would want to share these kinds of problems with anyone? In actuality, my problems were already under my control, but I just hadn't realized it and, at a deeper level, perhaps didn't want to: my guilt wouldn't allow it.

I have read statistics that indicate that as many as seventy-five to eighty percent of people experiencing extreme loss subsequently experience intense episodes of either panic or anxiety. Disturbingly, many of those people go without any kind of medical evaluation or understanding of what is happening inside themselves; they just tough it out. It's beyond confusing, but it is good practice to seek out information to determine whether or not what is being experienced is psychosomatic or an actual medical condition. Entangled in the throes of grief, I can truthfully say that I didn't care: what did it matter? However, at a deeper level, I felt some genuine relief that I was healthy. A part of me, in spite of my grief, still wants to live.

***

Recently, and quite unexpectedly, a memory surfaced from a time when I was in my early teens and playing little league baseball (not related to the train accident). I was generally a fairly good pitcher when I was playing, but for some reason, my coach had put me on second base and allowed another player to take the mound. The other pitcher was terrible and was, quite literally, throwing the ball over the backstop repeatedly. The score was 32-0, in the other team's favor, and I was becoming increasingly upset and angry as each inning passed. I finally reached a point where I just lost it. I threw my glove on the ground and started to walk off the field, refusing to play. My adopted Uncle was an assistant coach for our team and, becoming aware of my actions, immediately verbally stopped me in mid-step. He told me, in no uncertain terms, to get my ass back to base and play on. He said it didn't matter how I felt or what the score was; what mattered was that I said I wanted to play ball, and it would be ball that I would play. He told me, right there in front of everyone, that I had made a choice, and because I did, I would have to stick it out; quitting, giving up, was not an option. I stood there on the verge of rageful tears, turned around, went back to second base, picked up my glove and finished the game. I was not allowed to quit. Now, possibly due to that one incident, I will not quit of my own volition. I may be angry, I may be sad, I may not want to go on, but go on, I will. My Uncle and I had ups and downs in our relationship over the years but I appreciate the advice he gave me on that day and thank him for helping me become the man I now am.

As time progressed, I learned that despite my weaknesses, I would be able to care for and help Gloria. I would not and could not let her spend her time worrying about me (although, at times, I could not stop her from doing so). She loved me as much as I loved her. There were moments during the early stages of my anxiety when I actually found myself laughing out loud about my situation. Still, the humor never lasted for long: ten or fifteen minutes later, I would be ruminating about the fact that I most likely wasn't going to make it through the day. Her cancer of the liver was slowly eating away at my brain.

I now realize that one of the things that helped me the most to move through my fears was the act of facing and resolving the question of how I could deal with the brutal truth that she was dying and there was nothing I "could" do to avert it. For me, "could" was a nasty word because it implied that there really "could" be a way forward that I might have some control over. I had to learn that there was nothing I could do beyond loving her, which would change what we were facing. I had to learn that it is normal to be afraid. I had to learn that it is normal to lose sleep in the presence of her impending death. I had to learn to allow my experiences of anxiousness to come and go. I had to learn that it was okay to cry (sometimes uncontrollably), to feel hopelessness, to feel helplessness, and to feel depressed and sad. And I had to ask myself, who would not feel terrified and alone under the circumstances that Gloria and I were confronting. And finally, I had to learn that my marriage vows only qualified me to be a loving husband-forever. We loved each other until her death caused us to part:" I am not dead yet. We remain together.

***

Several years passed before a General Physician finally told me, directly, that I was suffering from anxiety attacks. I knew that, but I needed to hear it from the horses' mouth. It seems that many doctors of the body while recognizing that the mind does exist and is capable of creating illness, resist admitting to that fact. His offering of that truth seemed to calm me in some way, and since then, I have had fewer and fewer outright anxiety reactions. But when they do occur, they still run deep.

***

Gloria and I always saw life as an adventure, and we always recommended that others do the same. Even in our early years, we had a functioning car and our feet, and we used them to explore. When finances became more stable, we expanded our horizons. One of our greatest experiences was being able to tour Europe. We were able to visit and travel through multiple countries over a period of several weeks and formed memories that would remain with us forever. One very special moment came when we were visiting in the country of Italy.

Italy, Rome, and the Vatican were very powerful experiences for us due to their histories involving the development of Christianity. Gloria was raised Catholic, and being able to experience the Vatican, the very seat (more or less) of the first formal Christian expression, was awe-inspiring. We also walked around the now crumbling Coliseum, where gladiators were forced to fight one another to the death. Everywhere we went, we were surrounded by the history of the world. One of the most interesting aspects of our tour was a guided venture into the underground graveyard of the first Christians-the catacombs. Our descent into that dark, hallowed ground almost didn't happen, though, because Gloria had always had a fear of being trapped inside dark, closed spaces.

The catacombs are a complex of tunnels (passage ways) where the bodies of Christians were interred because the Romans would not allow believers in Christ to be buried on the surface. It is almost impossible to imagine that there are as many as 26 miles of tunnels, which were constructed and used for burial sites, stretching out beneath the city of

Rome. The tours offered are well-supervised and involve only a small portion of the entire network. Needless to say, it took a while for me to persuade Gloria to take the journey. I assured her I would be holding her hand and we would stay closely attached to the group we were with. Finally, after struggling with her own resistance, she stepped up to the edge of the entryway, took a few deep breaths, and down we went, entering into a world filled with endless rows of burial spaces, which were carved into the sides of the tunnels.

The tour was fascinating, and later, after we resurfaced and moved on, she expressed that descending into that sacred place was one of the most profound experiences she had ever experienced. She also qualified, with no hesitation, that she would never do anything like that again- just not her forte.

Following our time exploring Rome, we continued to Florence, Italy, and it was there that we were to discover another opportunity to form everlasting, wonderful memories. As we arrived at our hotel, we found ourselves totally exhausted and in need of a good night's sleep. We had decided that we would simply head to our room, bathe, and then pass out for the night. However, just prior to retiring for the evening, one of our tour guides informed us of a local restaurant located on a hill about a quarter mile from the hotel. He described the food as being some of the best in Italy, and the overall dining experience to be something that would produce lasting memories. I began thinking about the fact that we had not, in the past, nor would we, in the future, be wandering all over Europe. This world is a big place with lots to see. I suggested that the restaurant might just be the place to help us relax. Gloria, of course, was resisting. She was tired, and she didn't want to walk a long distance for any reason. And, of course, I was persisting.

I assured her that a quarter of a mile was not a difficult distance, and she might really enjoy herself (I was actually begging). And, to my excitement, she did not argue. For whatever reason, she gave in without any real resistance, and off we went. The path we followed was similar to a wide concrete sidewalk, and it was set on a gentle incline leading up a hill. We arrived, with only minimal effort, at the Ristorante Villa Vecchia. We immediately, and with great pleasure, noted that all the dining tables were located outside, and the eating area was decorated with a variety of multi-colored planters filled with beautiful blooming flowers. The weather was perfect. A waiter greeted us and guided us to a table where we were seated and presented with chilled bottled water, bread, and a delicious-tasting butter. Gloria was able to converse with the waiter in Spanish (which is very similar to Italian), and knowing that neither of us qualified as sophisticated wine drinkers, she requested a vino that would be sweet rather than dry. We were presented with a bottle of Orvieto Classico, which turned out to be a marvelous way to begin our meal.

The restaurant was set up buffet style and offered over fifty-five different food choices. The manner in which the food was arranged was pleasing to the eye and appeared to be meant just for us. We started with antipasto, then moved on to shrimp and pasta. The sauces were beyond belief in terms of flavor, and the linguini was something from another world. We ate, and ate, and ate, and enjoyed the moment like there was no tomorrow. Gloria tried their Astici alla Griglia (grilled lobster), while I went for Tounedos Rossini (filet mignon, smothered in mushroom and liver gravy). We finished our first bottle of Classico and then ordered a second. It goes without saying that by the end of our main meal, we were pleasantly inebriated. We decided to finish our dining experience with two different desserts: Gloria chose Torta Della Nonna (we had no idea what it was), and I ordered Zuppa Della Casa con Cioccolato (similar to a piece of cake with hot chocolate dripped on it). Both desserts were absolutely amazing, as they literally caressed our taste buds.

For two and a half hours, we ate, talked, drank wine, and watched other couples and families do the same. I still believe that our meal that evening was the most pleasant, relaxed dining experience either of us had ever had. The atmosphere was filled with love and enjoyment, and the experience itself, just as our guide said it would be, became permanently etched in our minds. It was an evening well spent. After finishing our dinner, we exited the restaurant, joined hands, and strolled back down the path that led to our hotel. In our room, tired but feeling fulfilled and at deep peace, we talked about making love. We stripped off our clothing, cuddled up naked in each other's arms and drifted off to sleep.

Chapter Fourteen
The Cough

"Oh child', spoke Papa tenderly,
"Don't ever discount the <u>wonder of your tears.</u>
<u>They can be healing waters and a stream of joy.</u>
<u>Sometimes they are the best words the heart can speak."</u>

Wm Paul Young-The Shack

In addition to her NASH diagnosis, there was one more medical concern (which I have previously briefly alluded to) that Gloria had to face and come to grips with: THE COUGH. In March of 2015, almost two years after her NASH diagnosis, for no apparent reason, she developed what became a chronic cough. When the cough first surfaced, a number of different medical problems seemed to arise simultaneously in association with it: hiccups (non-stop), a sore throat, vomiting, diarrhea, dehydration and then…coughing.

Her health providers considered none of these issues to be directly related to NASH. The hiccups were quickly resolved with a dose of Thorazine (strange to me, but true). The sore throat was treated initially with a Z-PAK. Still, after 48 hours of no throat relief, she saw a second doctor (because her primary doctor was not available) and that doctor prescribed additional antibiotics on top of the original prescription (despite being aware that the first prescription was only two days into her system). The more is better approach, I guess. Gloria trusted the recommendation, while I worried that guess work was probably being engaged in.

It was during the time that the hiccups, the cough, and the sore throat were being treated that she began experiencing frequent gagging and the vomiting of large amounts of phlegm. She then developed a high fever, which resulted in admission to the hospital with a severe case of "dehydration." After 4 days of treatment for dehydration and low sodium levels associated with it, those symptoms were resolved, and she was discharged to home. The cough, however, remained, and no explanation for its presence could be discerned.

The cough was not continuous, and onset would occur without warning. The episodes were physically draining, involving exhausting periods of retching and throwing up. Referrals were made to an endless list of "specialists" who, after running every kind of test, came up with one conclusion: "We have no idea of what might have prompted this problem." The coughing was not asthma-related, nor was it due to a lung condition. Blood analysis failed to show any abnormalities that might explain it. They didn't know what caused it, and they had no idea of how to correct it. We both had to learn to "just live with it."

Over the next few years, every relative and every friend who was either directly aware of the problem or had heard about it, would offer us their own insights, opinions, and possible solutions for it. I, myself, had never really had any experience with, nor knowledge of, medical conditions involving chronic coughing. We appreciated the flow of information from so many well-meaning, caring individuals, but nothing worked. And "nothing" even included a narcotic cough syrup, which was prescribed to her by her primary physician. Gloria, at first, balked about taking the syrup, worrying that she might become dependent upon it. Her physician, however, assured her that the dosage being recommended would not result in dependency and it might even calm her to a point where she could relax at night and improve her sleeping.

Over a period of time, it became evident to both of us that her primary physician, whom we respected and admired, had become mildly fixated on finding a solution to her problem. And, to our amusement (his included), during one of our scheduled visits, he told us that he was going to "go out on a limb" and recommend something different for her cough. He then, with some hesitation, suggested that she try a mixture of honey and lemon (a common household remedy for colds with coughing). All three of us were quiet for a moment, and we then all burst out laughing. It is amazing what "going out on a limb" can entail. Once we regained our composure, Gloria informed him that she had already been down that road with no success.

Vomiting was, by far, the most disturbing aspect of Gloria's coughing spells. Over time, we found that such episodes usually occurred directly following meals consumed in the mid-to-late afternoon. She absolutely hated to throw up. She was terrified and embarrassed by her loud gagging and retching response, and she was absolutely mortified by the thought that she might do so in a public setting, which, thankfully (especially for her), she never did. There were, though, a few occasions while having dinner in restaurants when she had to rush, as quickly as she could, without bringing attention to herself, to a bathroom to let it all go. The throwing up always seemed to drain her of her energy. A happy, relaxed moment could be erased in a flash by the psychological and physical impact of going through one of her episodes. And, counter to what we might have thought about her overall health, her initial stages of cancer turned out to be far less intrusive on her overall quality of life than was the ongoing presence of her cough. And, it was her cough that actually prompted her to think twice about attendance at many different normal social activities: school functions involving our grandchildren, going to movies, going to the theatre, the Bocelli Concert (mentioned in an earlier chapter), and being out in public, in general.

As time passed and the cough continued, we came to an uneasy acceptance of its presence (we had no choice). We graciously fended off well-meaning solutions, and, over time, we decided against further testing efforts. I maintained an ongoing search for new information on treating persistent coughs but always came up empty. I will say, in defense of my being persistent, that I am a devoted keeper of journals, and I maintained an ongoing record of each of her vomiting episodes and her eating habits just prior to their occurrence. I was actually able to identify specific food items that served to irritate her stomach and trigger her throwing up. This became helpful when ordering food from a restaurant menu and/or making homemade meals. It also provided me with the illusion that I was doing something meaningful.

Her episodes of coughing, to this day, have remained a mystery to me. Was it the increased dosage of antibiotics (maybe too much too soon), or was it related to one of her endoscopic procedures (which I haven't mentioned) involving, perhaps, the accidental irritation of the nerves lining her esophagus? Endoscopies, which were considered non-invasive, were performed on a routine basis for some time following her initial NASH diagnosis to prevent bleeding in the throat (bleeding that could lead to her death). The procedures required a light sedative and seemed to have no adverse side effects. She was fearful of the procedures at first, having a tube inserted into her throat while being awake, but gradually was able to tolerate them without problem. The procedure itself involved placing rubber bands around enlarged veins in her throat to prevent bleeding related to her diagnosis of NASH. The procedures were short, and she was able to walk out of the hospital without pain or complications shortly after their completion. I suppose, in my mind, an endoscopy procedure might have been the most likely culprit in triggering her cough and subsequent vomiting episodes. I wondered if a nerve in her throat had been scratched or damaged. Of course, her doctors rejected that idea and came to the expected conclusion that "she just coughs." In the end it makes no difference-it was just a thought.

The basic bottom line here is that after she had been diagnosed with a terminal disease, which is disturbing enough as if to add insult to injury, she began experiencing side-issues of chronic coughing and vomiting. Those episodes were so intense that they frequently caused muscle contractions in her upper back and shoulders and a lot of anxiety as she dashed for nearby bathrooms. She was often exhausted from the pain and discomfort of violent retching, and she had a sense of deep embarrassment (even around me) due to her loud gagging and throwing up. I always told her that her vomiting didn't bother me, and I always made sure that I was right there with her during every one of those moments, assuring her that she would be okay. Finally, as an aside, I should mention that for some unknown reason, the prescription of the scheduled narcotic cough syrup, which never seemed to impact her cough, was maintained for her use throughout the remainder of the years she had to live. I suggested to her that she just say no to it, but she decided to continue its usage. Later, even if she had become psychologically addicted to it, saying no was no longer important.

Gloria was, at her core, a strong, positive person, but her cough, unpredictable and intense, frequently disrupted her ability to sleep at night, and she was often overwhelmed and unrested. Her sleep, and mine, became totally erratic, sometimes to the point where neither of us was sleeping more than three or four hours a night. We were both, on an ongoing basis, physically and mentally overwhelmed, sleep-deprived, depressed, anxious, and irritable.

It was the extreme severity of two of her coughing/vomiting episodes that resulted in my need to alter my own normal daily routines for an extensive time and served to exaggerate my levels of anxiety to much higher degrees than I was normally used as her cancer progressed. In both of those instances, she would, without warning, lapse into intense coughing spasms which presented differently than what we had become accustomed to.

During the first bout, which took place in our home, while she was rushing to the bathroom to vomit, she suddenly collapsed to the floor, gasping for air and choking (this type of reaction had never occurred before). I immediately ran to her, got her back up on her feet, and lifted her hands and arms into the air to allow her to breathe. For a brief moment, I thought she was going to choke to death right there on the spot. It literally scared the hell out of me. Gradually, as her breathing normalized, she regained her composure and headed into the bathroom, where she vomited into the toilet, bringing that episode to an end. I now believe that her falling was the beginning of a panic attack, something she had not openly experienced before and would never admit to. I also believe that she was aware of that possibility but made no attempt to verbalize it.

The second episode (there were only two) happened in Ft. Worth, in the home of my younger daughter, Heather. One evening, as we sat watching television, Gloria, without any warning, started a severe bout of coughing. She quickly stood up, cupped her hands over her mouth, and started moving toward the bathroom. Once again, her legs seemed to give out from beneath her, but this time, I was right with her, reaching out, steadying her and keeping her upright: she didn't fall. I brought her arms above her head, and she was then able to gain control of her breathing and her focus. At that point, she moved under her own power to the bathroom and vomited into the toilet.

After she calmed down, she and I talked for a long

period of time about her feelings about what was happening in her life. I was letting myself assume a clinical approach with her (which I rarely ever did) as I explained to her that I could feel her ongoing struggle to keep her anxiety and fear under control. She, as I expected, did not accept the word anxiety. I accepted that and continued to talk with her about her need to somehow find the inner strength to overcome whatever unwanted thing was coursing through her mind. I also focused with her on the fact that even though her cancer was still below the radar and not impacting her day-to-day physical abilities, her cough and vomiting were. I purposefully suggested to her that she was going to have to keep fighting-she could not give in-and she could not give up. I was tapping into her underlying anger, pushing her to keep herself alive and functional. She didn't like our conversation, and she repeatedly told me that she did not like the word anxiety, although she had no other term to describe her feelings: she was just scared. I knew then that my efforts were paying off. And at the same time, I also knew that I was not only talking with her-I was also talking to myself.

It was specifically the two above-described incidents that convinced me that I could no longer leave her alone for any length of time. My bicycle riding, my golfing, my long walks with my dog, and other activities would have to come to an end. I worried continuously that she might collapse and choke to death in my absence. I told myself, while on necessary outings, that "staying in shape" and enjoying myself would become things of the past. I had visions of her lying on the floor, gasping for air, taking her last breath, and it would be my fault. My own anxiety, which was beginning to lessen in intensity prior to these two incidents, seemed to be on the rebound once again. Following her second incident, however, she never again responded to her coughing/vomiting episodes in the manner just described above.

However, my routines at that point were completely disrupted, and they have remained so to this day. Gloria's reactions, in collapsing, were very likely unconscious fear of death responses. She was physically losing control while, at the same time avoiding, mentally or verbally, what was going on in her mind. We were like two peas-in-a-pod in our inability to openly face our inner feelings. She finally did, though, especially with me, reach a point where she could talk about her fears, and there were moments with hospice nurses when she expressed being afraid of pain and what would happen to her as she died. I, on the other hand, kept my insecurities and fears to myself. It wasn't until I participated in a grief group and then wrote this book that I really began to open up to myself and the depths of my feelings.

***

I still cry almost every day, but I do so almost always in private. I did cry deeply and unreservedly in my first involvement with Grief Group members (five men and two women who cried right along with me). Crying has been a painful, agonizing experience: it has hurt, both physically and mentally. As time has passed, the physical hurt has become less intense, but I still feel it throughout my entire body when the tears start to flow. I fully understand that there are important reasons for crying, but crying does not necessarily have to be in the presence of others. It is absolutely necessary, I believe, for healing to take place. I see it as a baptism into a new life, a release from agony, a rebirth. In my mind, I am being bathed in a river of tears, bringing me to a new life. I have also come to understand that, in order for healing to occur, I must go through my grief rather than around it: such cannot be avoided.

I will say that it bothers me now, at least at times, to find myself still crying as much as I continue to do. I really thought that I would be feeling less emotional as time has passed, but I still have intensely painful moments. I have come to accept that my thoughts about Gloria's passing and my grief over it must be expressed to others. My feelings must, if they are to be effectively released, be heard by others, regardless of whether they are understood or not. The speaking part of grief is the most difficult of all the undertakings those experiencing it must go through. My refusal to reveal my sorrow was a reflection of my denial of her death. I could only talk about her at a superficial level, pretending to be "getting along." Writing this book has been difficult but it helps me in overcoming my need for someone to just listen-even if it's just myself. If you are now reading this, you are also listening.

Closing myself off and avoiding communication and genuine interaction with others is something I am working diligently to overcome. At times, I think I must appear to not want to interact with others. That would be both true and a misinterpretation. I want to have contact, but I have not sought interactions simply because they hurt too much. To interact is normal, and I certainly have not felt "normal" for a long time. Ultimately though, life is too short for avoidance. Making contact has been a difficult struggle for me to undertake as I reawake to the world around me-a world I had lost sight of. At the same time, though, being alone has also been truly important and necessary for me. Jesus was alone in the desert, facing the meaning and purpose of his life. Others have not, and still do not, understand that. Buddha, for 40 days, sat beneath the Bodhi Tree, confronting his own meaning and purpose in the presence of suffering and death. There are times when I appear to be pulling away from others, and they become worried about me. They think being alone is unhealthy. Definitely a misinterpretation.

I have also found that when my loved ones, or those who are focused on helping me, find that I am "having bad moments," their most obvious response is that I should find ways to keep myself busy. The fact is, I cannot stay busy twenty-four hours a day, even if I wanted to (which I don't). And, for me, there really is no such thing as flat-out downtime. If I sit for an hour in meditation (which I often do), I am doing something: I am busy meditating. At least once every day, I am busy sleeping (or trying to sleep). Rarely have close friends or relatives ever suggested to me that I might consider meditating for an hour or getting some sleep as a way to stay busy. Why would that be? I know people who are incapable of sitting quietly or sleeping for five minutes (their minds are too busy). I believe the concept of "busy" is in the mind of the beholder.

With Gloria's death always walking beside me, I have found that the early evening hours of each day are my most relaxed. This has remained true for me, even now. In thinking about this, I have realized that even though I am retired, I still focus on the daytime hours as being those hours when I have to be "productive," (busy). Additionally, Gloria and I were more active and moving during the day, while during the evening and nighttime, we were relaxing. Relaxing, as I perceive it, is not downtime. Rather, it is refocusing on something I want to do as opposed to something I have to do. Therefore, I am busy until I fall asleep (when I get busy sleeping). When the "workday" comes to an end, I am ready to get busy relaxing.

I, generally, experience a sense of peace and quiet as late afternoon begins to settle in. I certainly would not attempt to write a book like this in the evening (way too busy). When darkness begins to settle in, I find myself ruminating less and focusing more on reading, television, playing my guitar, and exploring other areas of interest. This is my version of "keeping myself busy." I guess what I'm saying here is that most of the advice I receive is not really directed toward staying busy. Rather, it is focused on the idea of having fun and trying to avoid that which is unavoidable. It is like being given a suggestion that if I stop breathing, I'll feel better. I really am getting better at having moments of genuine fun, but doing so is still difficult. I still find myself questioning whether I should be having fun. I'm not quite there yet, but I'm working on it. What I can say is that I can be fairly assured that I will sleep well and will awake the next morning with a positive attitude (at least for a while). I understand that my positive attitude may not last forever, but it is helpful in building healing power over time.

Chapter Fifteen
Coming to Peace with my God

Your daily life is your temple and your religion.
Whenever you enter into it take with you your all...

Kahlil Gibran-The Prophet

I have slept well, better than the last few nights, and have awakened with a sense of contentment. Luke, who has his own bed, is stirring. He is aware that I am about to rise up and start the day. Today, I find myself thinking about how it used to be for Gloria and me when we had an established morning routine to begin each new day. Once up and moving around, we would make our bed, dress, brush our teeth, and then head to the kitchen. The Keurig is an amazing invention. Within a few minutes, coffee in hand, a pair of birding binoculars draped around my neck, and several bird guides resting precariously in my other hand, we would head to our back porch, where chairs and a small table awaited us. Luke would be right there with us, first bounding into the yard, moving one way, then the other, sniffing, licking, and surveying, hoping to encounter an unwary cat or squirrel. After assuring himself that there was nothing of immediate concern to harass, he would return to the porch and lie close to us, head up and eyes alert to the surrounding area, waiting for unsuspecting opportunities. We both believed, without doubt, that he saw all this as part of his personal kingdom.

We both loved plants and over the years, we slowly turned our back porch into a plant heaven. We surrounded ourselves with lush hanging Ivies, Spider Plants, Snake plants, Geraniums, Lantanas, Sage, Lemon Grass, Mosquito plants, various cacti, Gardenia, and whatever else we thought might thrive in extreme Texas weather. We accepted the fact that bone-chilling winters and drought-ridden summers would potentially kill what we so lovingly, in the good weather, tended to. We brought in a small swinging seat for people to relax in as they gently rocked back and forth. We positioned chairs and small tables in strategic viewing areas, and we set up an umbrella-covered table for sharing meals with family and friends. The entire porch was covered with ceramic frogs, birds, angels, and Dia De Los Muertos items of variegated colors. And, for nighttime social activities, we strung soft lights and citronella torches along the railing. It was beautiful, and very peaceful: something we created, reflecting our hearts; it felt like heaven on earth.

Over the span of many years, we held birthday parties, social events, and quiet gatherings in our backyard, and we cherished the comforting gatherings produced there. Oftentimes, there was music and dancing (which wasn't easy on a wooden porch), and lots of conversation, laughing, and just being together. Many times, when Gloria and I were by ourselves, I would bring out my guitar and sing for her in the quiet of the evening. And, there were nights when we just sat together, by ourselves, and talked and enjoyed the darkness and the sound of the surrounding silence. And the years flew by. Our back porch morning routine continued on until about one month prior to Gloria's dying. As the cancer grew more aggressive, her ability to move around became more difficult, and she needed more time for simply stretching out and resting. During her last month, lying on the couch in our living room, she would peer through our French door windows, scanning the yard for the birds she loved.

The ritual on our back porch had become a permanent part of our lives following our respective retirements from the work world: she retired several years before I did. We were very familiar with the wildlife in our area, and our "library" of birding books, as we sat watching our feeders, was not essential beyond identifying the rare appearance of some winged creature we had not viewed before. On one occasion, we were privileged to observe a Mississippi Kite (not at all common to our area) perched high in a tree, surveying the sky and visually exploring the foliage and ground beneath him, hoping for a meal to present itself. A magnificent bird; he sat unmoving, allowing me time to retrieve my camera and take multiple pictures of him for well over an hour. Finally, with no food to be had, he stretched his wings and lifted into the air to resume his journey. Regular visitors to our feeders included Cardinals (Cardinals appear when angels are near), Blue Jays, Finches, Chickadees, Painted Buntings, and a host of others. Gloria and I would sit for lengthy periods of time just watching.

We also hung Hummingbird feeders along the outside rafting of the overhead to our porch to draw in the yearly migration of Hummers intent on their journey to Mexico or South America and needing a resting point along the way. Hummingbird movement through our area of Texas is, generally, from the beginning of July through mid-September. There were many days during that span of time when we would sit and watch as many as twenty-five to thirty Hummers competing for spots on our feeders. And we learned that if we stood quietly beneath the feeders and extended a forefinger up to the feeding spots, these tiny birds would land on them and feed without any signs of fear.

My mind, as I write, had suddenly leaped back many years ago to a time when Gloria and I, moving around in our backyard, had decided to bring down a dying oak tree before it toppled against our house. Using my chainsaw, I quickly cut through it, and it came crashing to the ground, scattering dried and broken branches and twigs in all directions. As we began to clean-up, we became aware of a nest of Bluejay eggs lying on the ground next to the debris. Miraculously, the eggs were intact-none broken. And, at the very moment of our discovery, we heard a violent shrieking above our heads and looked up to see a female Bluejay diving toward the nest and frantically streaking by. She was screeching (screaming) as she flew back and forth, over and over again. We could feel the terror and fear issuing from the cries she was emitting. We actually thought she might attack us, but she didn't. Eventually, she just disappeared. We knew that we had unwittingly destroyed her home and disturbed her unborn babies, and we felt terrible and sad about it. We also were aware that if we touched the nest or the eggs, the mother might not return: but we felt that we had to do something to right the situation. Carefully, using a thin piece of plywood to slide beneath it, we managed to pick the nest up and relocate it to a crook in a branch of another tree. That was the only option we had. We were unsure about the outcome but hoped the babies would somehow survive. At that moment we understood that grief, in no way, is limited just to human beings.

Our backyard was (and is to this day) a magnificent rendering of nature's beauty. Oak and Cedar trees provided us with a natural boundary between our home and the homes of our neighbors, and God took care of the land we lived on. I mowed and trimmed while God chose to water or not. We were surrounded by every shade of green and brown imaginable to the human mind. And, with the onset of spring, the wildflowers would rise from the earth, cover the ground, drink from the sun and rain, and bless us with their beauty, then disappear to wait for the next year to begin the cycle again. Gloria and I, sitting quietly together, watching the world around us, knew that we were in heaven and we were surrounded and comforted by the love of God.

***

Grief rendered me helpless in the presence of my Lord: who was with me and all around me at all times (despite my crippling inability to interact with it). Gloria's death ripped my soul in two and brought me to my knees, rendering me unable to right myself. Our porch remains, but my sorrow has clouded my ability, until very recently, to return to the ritual of sitting and being with nature in Gloria's absence. My grief has thrust me into a state of numbness and has forced me to explore, at the deepest level, my understanding of the meaning and presence of God in my life. In returning to those moments when Gloria and I spent precious time on our porch, watching life come and go, I have reached a point where being with God (my God) has become unquestionably essential to my survival in this world.

As I have mentioned, Gloria was raised in the Catholic religion. I, on the other hand, was simply raised. My maternal Aunt and my maternal Grandmother expressed a belief in God, but they never really discussed what they believed with me. I really don't think they could. The closest thing to a "religious" discussion, as I grew up, came in the form of sentences like, "You'd better behave because God is watching you." "Really," I would think, while maybe glancing at the blue, gray, or black sky above. The only time we ever went to church was during the celebration of Easter, which my sisters and I associated with new shoes and a new set of school clothes. I did go to church at times with friends, but never attended anything even closely related to bible classes. My early religious experiences were basically social in nature and were always fun or cautionary. Much later, in Vietnam, we had a saying; "Kill em all and let God sort em out." After we married, Gloria and I attended church irregularly but never committed ourselves to routine participation (my problem, not hers). Life went on until one day when our daughter, Celeste, with no conscious intention, served to be the impetus for bringing my views on the idea of a higher power into clear focus.

Celeste was close to five years old when it was recommended to us that she have her tonsils removed. Tonsillectomy, in that era of medicine, was a common practice for reducing (supposedly) the number of colds and sore throats children experienced on a regular basis around that early age. Gloria and I discussed it and decided that it made sense. On the day of her operation, however, what we thought was going to be a routine procedure turned out to be a nightmare. As we sat patiently waiting for the simple surgery to be completed, we found ourselves being approached by a hospital Chaplain. He introduced himself and asked if we would mind accompanying him into the chapel, where we could sit and talk with him. A red flag immediately rose in both our minds. I looked at Gloria, then turned and asked him outright if something was wrong. He attempted to skirt the issue and again requested that we join him in the chapel, where we could talk in private. At that point, I politely said no and indicated to him that if something was wrong, we could talk about it right where we were sitting. Resignedly, he then explained to us that the procedure had gone well, but the doctors were having trouble stopping her from bleeding in her esophagus: they were worried that she might not make it. My immediate response was to become anxious and agitated. Gloria seemed to be in shock and became quiet. The Chaplain again encouraged us to move into the chapel with him. I indicated to Gloria I could not enter the chapel and I needed to get outside: I needed to move and breath.

In hindsight, I think Gloria might have agreed with the Chaplain, but she could see how upset I was and agreed to move outside for a few minutes so I could walk and get control of myself. Out the door, we went, with a sense of dread spreading throughout our entire being. We walked, saying nothing. I studied the clouds in the sky and the trees and grass surrounding the hospital and took in deep breaths of air, and, gradually, I began to feel myself beginning to calm. Within a few minutes, I had regained my composure and was focused enough to agree to go back into the hospital and relocate to the chapel. The Chaplain accompanied us as we seated ourselves in a hard wooden pew and then indicated he would check on Celeste and return with more information. As Gloria and I sat there, staring ahead at a statue of Jesus on a cross, I began to experience a strange, not unpleasant sensation. A force (for lack of a better description) began to settle at the top of my head.

Slowly, a powerful, soothing energy began flowing down through my body, reaching to the very bottoms of my feet: it covered me in a complete sense of calm and wellbeing. I felt myself become completely relaxed, and my worry for my little girl, my baby, simply disappeared. My fear was gone. I looked at Gloria, described to her what was happening inside me, and told her that whatever would transpire, it would be as it should be-whether or not she lived or died. I questioned Gloria about her own feelings, but she was still trying to process what was happening and fearing the possible loss of our child. She was praying. I explained to her that the essence of God (the only words I could come up with) had entered into me and I understood that whatever would happen was beyond either of our control. A few seconds after my epiphany, the chaplain returned and informed us that the bleeding in Celeste's throat had ceased, and the doctors felt she was recovering well and would be fine. Oddly, over the many following years of our life together, that experience, that knowledge, would quietly recede from my conscious awareness. It had become dormant but has now resurfaced, and I am beginning to define the true nature of my belief.

I do believe in the concept of God, but I do not believe in the existence of a conscious God. I do believe in Jesus.

For me, Jesus was and is a beautiful, compassionate, caring, loving human being who was crucified for his resistance to the hypocrisy of Orthodox Judaism. I do not believe that Jesus was a God (I guess you might say that I am a Christian deist). I do believe that He (Jesus) is my Savior in the sense that His message of love is the only pathway leading to eternal life and human salvation. Also, the ideas of heaven and hell are of importance in the manner in which I address daily existence. I have talked briefly, elsewhere in this book, about the issue of how everything we do is survival-oriented. As conscious human beings, all of us are engaged in creating optimal conditions for our ongoing existence as living beings. I seek to create heaven on earth for myself, my family, my friends, and for others, human or non-human, for the purpose of enhancing my ability to survive and prosper in life. My day-to-day interactions with my job, my home, and the things I surround myself with all represent what I call heaven. Heaven is that place where I am at peace and in harmony with life in general. Heaven is where love is nourished and strengthened. I create (or at least attempt to create) my heaven. Hell, on the other hand, is anything that interferes with my vision of what heaven should be.

Hell is sickness, physical threat, loss, and death. In general, I do not take responsibility for creating Hell, and I will do whatever I can to offset or correct that which represents a threat to the heaven I seek. My survival, my life and the life of those I love is what existence is all about. When Gloria died, I slipped into a state of Hell. Gloria and I were one, and her death was my death, and my death was the death, also, of my heaven. I now understand, though, that my heaven was not destroyed, but it was severely compromised. My life was compromised, and returning to life has been, to say the least, an almost impossible journey. Jesus is my guide and teacher as I return to life.

And finally, I believe that the Bible, in whatever form it is presented, is a metaphorical expression rather than a reality-based reflection of actual life. I have taken the time to read the Bible, from cover to cover, twice, while most people I know have never read it even once. I fully recognize that it (both Old Testament and New) abounds with a profound knowledge of what I must do to fulfill my brief time here on earth. And all this is what I carried with me as I entered into my first grief group experience following Gloria's death. While sitting in that group, I recognized that my interpretation of what it entails to be a Christian is not a traditional viewpoint; it is my viewpoint. I am thankful that the leaders of my group, regardless of their own orientations, were focused on each grievers' individual understanding, as opposed to their own. This is, in fact, why I chose a non-denominational group setting.

I knew, following Gloria's passing, that a time would come when I would seek out a situation where I could share my grief with others who, like me, were struggling with their own losses. My grown children were working and raising my grandchildren, and they could not be available for "counseling" me through my feelings of devastation. They could help at times, but I needed something that could reach my core. It turned out to be several months before I was able to bring myself to join the grief group process. Planning a Celebration of Life, interacting with insurance companies, addressing changes in credit-related issues, and whatever else might come up was an exhausting, frustrating, time-consuming process. And I had no interest or desire to go out looking for "new friends" of any kind. I frequently found myself just wanting to be left alone (stuck in place). Complicating matters even further was the fact that I was not interested in affiliating with any highly organized religious organization, nor was I looking for "direction" in how I SHOULD address Gloria's death, according to the Word of God. What I wanted was a non-judgmental interaction with other people who were experiencing deep pain and confusion due to tragedy in their own lives and were willing to openly discuss their feelings. I was looking only to engage in an atmosphere of sharing, and through that sharing, I hoped I would come to recognize the answers I was searching for. I was also very sensitive to the fact that grief group and bible study are not the same. After carefully exploring group options available in my area, I chose to attend a non-denominational group, which met on a once-weekly basis.

As I arrived for our first meeting, I felt more like a zombie than a human being. Sitting there, struggling with the urge to leave, I quickly realized that I was immersed in a group of six men and two women. The women were both Pastors and group leaders and were both dealing with their own issues of loss or death. I felt as if I was being crushed by a heavy blanket of sadness, pushing down and constricting the air around me. After a brief welcome, each participant (including the leaders), one by one, was asked to share with the others our reasons for joining the group. Tears were steadily flowing as we went from one person to the next around the room, and when my turn arrived, I found myself unable to speak. I tried, but I feared that I would simply break into an endless episode of uncontrollable sobbing, so I asked to be temporarily passed over. My request was granted, and other members continued to share their reasons for being present. Of course, the attention finally returned to me, and after inhaling what I thought might be my last breath, tears gushing from my eyes, I explained that Gloria, my wife of 53 years, had passed away a few months earlier, on New Years Eve, day. I need to add here that this group was the church's first all-male group (other than the two leaders), and it was a gift to me and the others, as well, that we were all, at the same time, crying and confronting not only our own loss but each other's loss, also. I somehow survived that first meeting and, over time, I developed lasting friendships with those whom I shared my sorrow with.

One of the first topics of discussion, following our introductions to one another, turned to the question of whether or not we were angry with or blaming God for the death of our loved ones (as I have previously alluded to). Did we attribute responsibility for the circumstances which had resulted in a devastating loss in our lives on God? I saw the question as, "are you mad at God for your wife's death? My answer was simple and straightforward. I explained that my God did not kill people: my wife died of cancer. I then added, "I am not mad. I am sad." In talking about my belief that my God does not kill people, I cited disease, natural disasters, advanced normal aging, and people killing people as some of the reasons we die, none of which represents retribution from a higher power. As the discussion grew in depth, I offered my belief that Jesus did not save people from death on this earth; He rendered unto Ceasar that which was

Ceasar's. I offered that Jesus was subjected to crucifixion and, while being crucified, He did not grant the two "criminals" hung on crosses next to him a pass. They both underwent the horror of being nailed to the cross, just as He did. One of them, according to the Bible, went to Heaven, but I'm still not clear about what happened to the other. Long story short, Jesus, for me, is a messenger of love. He was a human being. He taught the message of Life and Death and spoke to us of our journey through the Valley of the Shadow. He was crucified by his brothers, not God. I found myself ministering and learning in the same breath.

As I entered deeper into the grief group process, sharing my thoughts and hurts with the other members, I began to actively join myself with what I see as the Jesus Within. I believe He lives within each of us, reaching out and offering love and support to all those who seek it. And, in that grief group, through the telling of the stories of my life with Gloria, He came alive within me to a level that I had never encountered before. I explained that I was alive and dead at the very same time. In response, the members of the group offered their love to me as they, in turn, shared their own stories of sadness and loss. I shared with them that my God, the God of Life and Death, is around me and within me, in everything I do and in every place I go, and Gloria is always with me: I see her, I talk to her, I walk with her, and I love her. I always will. She is in the trees, the clouds, and the sky, both night and day, and she will be there forever.

I had, without believing it would ever be possible, begun the process of healing. I thought it would never happen, that my future was doomed. But my hope within has come about because my Jesus Within surrounded me with his disciples, and they have ministered to me and offered healing through their love. I, in turn, have been there for others as well as they struggled to come alive once more. For a year, I remained in the grief group setting, and I grew strong enough (although it was difficult to impossible at times) to minister to others along the way while I continued to learn and grow.

Losing Gloria has taught me many things about the sanctity of life and my need to "resist my resistances," allowing myself to rejoice in simply BEING, once more. I will admit I have not yet reached a point where I am fully joined in life as I would want. But I know, as well, that the hardest things in life are often the greatest teachers.

***

When Gloria and I took our vows, we swore to each other that we would maintain our relationship through "better or worse, through sickness and health, until death do us part." The words "except," "if," or "but" were not a part of our commitment. We considered the bond we made to each other and to God to be permanent, and over the years, we extended our relationship to "forever." And, of course, through the passing of years, like all couples, we found that ups and downs in our interactions would put our commitment to the test. We sometimes argued intensely about our given points of view. There were times when we would become so irritated with one another that walking off, for some time, would be the only way to calm ourselves. But, through all our trials and tribulations, our disagreements, and our unwillingness to bend, we always

230

maintained and accepted our love for one another. And, strangely, along the way, we even found that our relationship could be a source of contention for many of the people we were closely associated with; both family and friends. We became sadly aware of the fact that many people consider the vows of marriage to be meaningless promises, representing nothing more than a traditional manner of expression, words empty of depth. We wondered: how do you promise something to God and then not carry out your word? Our word, and our job, is to create Heaven on earth. We eventually came to the conclusion that, just maybe, it comes down to a learning curve, and if we allow ourselves time, knowledge and understanding will come.

***

The bottom line in our disagreements always came down to the fact that when they would first begin, neither of us was strong enough to stop and take a deep breath. Neither of us was able to acknowledge the truth of the old adage, "It takes two to tango." We would raise our voices, point our fingers, and badger one another unmercifully. I would stomp off to the den, or she would retreat to the bedroom, both of us frustrated in that we had reached a stalemate rather than the "big win." So much for the picture-perfect couple. The bottom line for us, though, was that every time there was a battle, there also came a time and opportunity to make peace. In fact, if I may be so bold, we loved making peace. With peace came the understanding that in our conflicts, we were indeed doing the Tango instead of our preferred slow Two Step or a Waltz. We did love to dance.

It has been said that "love conquers all things," and

Gloria and I allowed that conquering to carry us above the frays in our ongoing relationship. Needless to say, we saw and interpreted things differently than those around us, but those differences seemed to bring us closer rather than creating barriers between us. There was no room for separation in our relationship; it could not happen. Laughingly, at times, she would look at me with a grin on her face and say something like, "You're a heathen." I always found those references to be funny and endearing because she knew my heart, and my heart was love, without question. Over our years of marriage, we both learned to open ourselves to different perceptions and ways of dealing with life and death. Our differences were truly our strengths. In my grief, I have rambled through memories of our discussions about God and what it has meant in our lives, both together and apart. I will now end this chapter with one final story that reflects and confirms (for me) the existence of "my God."

The year was 2020, and thousands of people were, daily, dropping dead as Covid spread unhindered throughout the United States. Human beings across the entire globe were in shock as the world around them disintegrated into fear and chaos. For those of us still living, life was becoming more and more complicated. We all had to work (if we still had jobs), and, more importantly, we all had to eat and eating required visits to grocery stores. Gloria, at the time of Covid, was still active but slowing down. Our doctors had repeatedly warned us that her immune system was becoming progressively more compromised. She needed to wear a mask in public, and she would be wise to avoid large crowds, including unprotected contact with other family members.

She and I quickly learned that we had to be especially wary of the "heroes" walking amongst us, refusing to wear protective masks.

One afternoon, while Gloria became comfortable in our car, I donned my mask and headed into the grocery store with a list of items I needed to buy. I was wearing my Vietnam Veteran cap, which always drew attention from people around me. Securing a shopping cart, which was a good reference source for purposes of distancing, I started down an aisle. I immediately became aware of an unmasked man, possibly in his mid-fifties, approaching me. He was nicely dressed, clean-shaven, and smiling as he extended his hand toward me, thanking me for my service. Normally, I wouldn't hesitate to engage in a handshake (it's a conditioned response), thank the person, and move on. Covid, however, had changed that routine. I looked at him, stepped behind my basket, and politely explained that the possibility of Covid kept me from handshaking. He halted his movement toward me, seeming to consider my statement, and then explained to me that he was a minister from one of the local churches. As he did so, he reached into his jacket side pocket and brought out a small cross. He extended his hand once again, offering the cross as he expressed that it would be his gift to me. I paused and politely indicated to him that I could not accept gifts from strangers. I told him that I did not mean to be rude but was protecting my wife, who was suffering from terminal liver cancer and could not risk Covid infection from exposure to unmasked people or contact with items that were not sanitized. He stood there looking at me, seeming to consider the information I had provided him with, and then replied, "You don't even accept a gift from a church?" Calmly, I responded, "No, not even from a church." With a shrug of his shoulders and a look of disbelief in his eyes, he turned and walked away. The Church of Satan flashed through my mind.

Thank God he went on to greener pastures. I am not, apparently, acquainted with his God, but I can say, without any hesitation, that my God does not abide by one of His disciples turning away from those in need, even when they are not asking for help. He seemed put off, offended, by my calm resistance to his offerings and, interestingly to me, he never made any attempt to pause, step back a bit, think, and ask me how either I or my wife were handling our situation. He never suggested that she be put on his church's prayer list. He just walked away. In that brief moment my God had sent me a powerful message. I came away knowing that joining this man's congregation would never be a consideration. I sincerely hope, for the sake of his parishioners, that his church refrains from offering grief group sessions.

Chapter Sixteen

Gloria's Song

If in the twilight of memory, we should meet once more, we shall speak again together and you shall sing me to a deeper song.

Kahlil Gibran-The Prophet

My personal experiences with grief have always reflected two sides of expression: private and public. The private parts surface in the forms of ongoing, unrelenting anxiety, unexpected waves of intense crying, excruciating episodes of body pain, feelings of weakness (I can't go on), and a reluctance to engage with life (any life) "out there." At the beginning of Gloria's battle with cancer and following her death, I had no desire to share my disturbing thoughts and feelings with others: to include grief group members, with whom I chose to be open with, and in spite of my need to do so. The public side of my grief involved my ability to create a façade while in the presence of others: family, friends and acquaintances. I suspect that those who are most familiar with me were, for the most part, able to see through my cover-up and then had to decide how they would respond to it. They could recognize when I was "faking it, to make it," and they could sense, within themselves, my subtle discomfort in being around people in general. Humans, whether we think so or not, are very nuanced in terms of reading one another's feelings and moods.

At times, when I have concluded that I am getting better and having more "normal" moments, such recognition would almost certainly result in later regressions. Anxiety, for instance, is something I seem to hold on to, almost as though I'm reserving it to correct my thinking (which might include feeling good). I like to say it that way because by doing so I am indicating to myself that I do have control over such reactions and I need to exercise it. Crying in private has remained with me and can serve as a major distraction at times, although I accept it as being natural. When I cry, I am missing Gloria at the deepest of levels. However, I recognize my crying to be, more so than any other emotional factor I have experienced, the mechanism by which I am able to release the pain, fear, and sadness that has settled into my being, following Gloria's death. I find myself encouraged by the increase of better moments I experience, but I still find myself wondering how long the good times will last. The process of grief has been much longer and more difficult than I ever thought it would be. I would like to think that I no longer feel guilty about feeling good, but even there, there are painful exceptions.

In thinking back over the past two years, I can bring to memory only a few times when I have broken down sobbing in front of others. One of those times occurred when Gloria's older brother and his wife were visiting with me after her death. During a conversation with them, while sitting at our kitchen table, I simply broke down and started crying. I cried and cried until there were no more tears. It was horrible and uplifting, all at the same time.

A second memory of deep crying in front of others

occurred in my dining room several weeks after Gloria's passing when the Hospice Chaplain and the Nurse, who regularly monitored her spiritual and medical condition, dropped by to see how I was doing. I was not expecting their visit but was quite pleased that they were willing to spend time with me.

As we sat around the dining room table the Chaplain inquired as to how I had been handling myself since losing Gloria. As I started to reply, my words turned to tears. I became speechless and just sat there, unable to speak, my pain flowing from my eyes. The Nurse, who was quietly listening, stood up, came directly to me, wrapped her arms around me, and she began crying as well. This was a hospice nurse who interacted with the dying every day. She sometimes sat with them, soothing them as they passed from this world. I knew she had emotions, but I did not expect to see her express them in front of or for me. As our moment of sorrow slowly passed, she explained to me that Gloria was one of the braver souls she had ever encountered in her involvement with the terminally ill. She expressed that she was always amazed at how Gloria had maintained her sense of humor and her willingness to confront her situation head-on, without anger or acting out, a problem she frequently encountered with other terminally ill patients. She had felt close to Gloria and had answered questions for her about her fear of dying. I was appreciative and thankful for every word coming from her mouth. I truly believe that death is harder for those who survive it, as opposed to those succumbing to it, especially dedicated caregivers.

I know in my heart that those people who have been

closest to me since Gloria's death are still painfully aware of my continuing grief, especially in relationship to my obvious uneasiness (and theirs as well) in matters of social interactions, with either immediate family or close acquaintances (I have discussed this earlier). I also have learned that grief has no rules; grief is what grief is. There is no schedule to follow in terms of healing. I'm not going to just get over it. Grief is the mind and body's way of righting themselves in the presence of overwhelming loss.

The world I now live in is no longer the world I shared with Gloria. The world that now surrounds me has taken on a different meaning and gone in a different direction without any say-so on my part. I can say that life truly does go on, and I am being reborn into a completely new reality that I do not know. I am literally going through a process of learning to live again. In doing so, I have come to recognize that there is wisdom in some of what people want for me, but I am traveling down a path on which none of them has yet to set foot. How could it be otherwise; they were not WE. They are creating their own lives. I know they suffer, but their suffering is (as is mine) tempered by their own individual need to continue on with life. Each of them has their own direction, their own goals, and their own purpose, and this truly is as it should be.

On the other hand, as each day passes, I am becoming aware and surprised by the fact that what I am now relearning is really no different than what I knew before (it is and it is not). So, I want those of you whom, in your eyes, I seem to have separated from to know that I love you and my new path will, in time, lead me back to you. I do miss you (even when we are together), and I know you miss me. I also know that you understand what I am saying, and you forgive me for my transgressions (real or imagined). I am winning the battle within myself to become strong again, and you must do the same.

***

Did you know that when you gaze at the stars at night, what you think you are seeing may not be there? For just a while longer, keep that strange thought in your mind.

When I was a boy attending elementary school, I developed an interest in astronomy. I decided to write to every observatory in the United States to solicit information about the countless stars, the universe, and the planets that surround this earth we live upon. I was pleasantly surprised to discover that every letter I wrote was promptly responded to. All the observatories wrote me back, offering me a never-ending stream of knowledge about the earth, the galaxy, and the expanse of seeming nothingness that stretches above us forever. There is no end to it, no wall to reach out to and touch, just emptiness. Subsequently, over a period of many years, I learned about the planets, the stars, the constellations, and the idea of what infinity might or might not mean. Nighttime, simply sitting and gazing upward, became a meditation for me. I would sit for hours, allowing my eyes to wander through the darkness, searching for a shooting star or piecing together the formation of a constellation. Star gazing became both calming and exciting at the very same moment.

Gloria, as she grew to adulthood, enjoyed being

outdoors and looking up at the night sky, but she, like most people, never sought to learn more about it. The night sky, for her, was a beautiful mystery but was left unexplored. After we married, I decided to introduce to her the magic of the heavens. I taught her how to recognize the constellations, the observable planets, and a number of the commonly known stars. As night came on and the darkness settled in, we would set up chairs in our front yard, and I would trace out each constellation with my star laser and then ask her to do the same. She absolutely loved it and gradually became independent in her ability to name what she was seeing. Satellites, silent minute dots, gliding through the heavens, and shooting stars were her favorite sightings. And along the way, WE also taught our grandchildren the wonders of stargazing, drawing them into it by first allowing them to play with my star laser, and then by having them point out and name the stars and planets above them. It became a game of show me the star, Spica, and you get fifty cents (or a piece of candy). The kids loved it, and they learned at the same time (and sometimes even made money in the process).

Gloria, through my telescope, saw the rings of Saturn, the gaseous clouds and moons of Jupiter, and the mountain ranges traversing Earth's moon. One of her all-time favorite activities was sitting outside during meteor showers, counting shooting stars, and having a contest with me to be the one who would see the most. And, on a couple of occasions, we even brought our cheapo barbeque grill into the front yard, threw on some wieners, and invited our neighbors and their children to star gaze with us.

One of the coolest things that Gloria could do was to

be able to pick out the North Star, Polaris, not only from our own front yard but also from various places in the United States where we had visited. In Big Bend National Park, for instance, she could stand in the middle of the darkened desert and point out directions by locating Polaris and moving out from there. To me, this was an amazing feat on her part because, in modern America, few adults can do the same. Two thousand years ago, children, sheepherders, and countless others used the position of the stars in the night sky to navigate, travel, plant crops, and harvest. Human survival, in those past times, depended on their knowledge of the stars. Modern man, however, is not so well informed. Several years ago, during a hunting trip in South Texas, I sat in the back of a pick-up truck with a group of hunters being transported to deer blinds. I casually asked if any one of them knew what direction we were traveling in. To my surprise, not one of the men sitting with me was able to answer my question. These men were intelligent, hard-working providers who hunted on a regular basis and yet knew nothing of the night sky. Modern technology had relieved them of their need to seek an understanding of the nature that surrounded them.

Now, let us return to my reference to the fact that when you look up at the stars twinkling high above you in the black of the night, some of those stars may not actually be there. What you and I are seeing as we gaze upward is very much like a memory (or perhaps an afterimage). At some time in the distant past, millions or billions (or maybe even trillions) of years ago, those celestial bodies we think we are seeing ceased to be. They died, but their light shines on. To understand how this can be, think about going outside one night with a flashlight in your hand and observing

Jupiter moving through the sky above you. If you shine your light at it, it takes somewhere between thirty-four to fifty minutes for it to travel from where you are to its final destination on Jupiter. Now, consider that when you direct your light toward the brightest star in the night, Sirius, it will take that light about nine years to travel from your location to it. It is strange to think that if you shined your light at Sirius when you were ten years old, someone living on that star (not likely) would actually receive the light at the time you were turning nineteen years of age. If, somehow, an image of you accompanied your light, the being receiving it would see you as a ten-year-old, not nineteen. Understanding this concept (which I don't), peer further into space, trillions and trillions of miles from where you stand, and imagine that distance as it relates to light reaching from it to you. When you look into space, you are literally looking at the past. The distance away from Earth determines how far back in time you are going. Needless to say, neither Gloria nor I were astronomers (lucky for astronauts) but WE were fascinated with the heavens which hovered above us.

In years past, as WE sat watching the stars, WE did not think about dying. WE were fully alive to one another and the heavens, stretching out forever above us. Gloria used to tell the grandkids, "I will love you to infinity and beyond," a phrase which our grand-children, in actuality, introduced to us. My grief has been an arduous (to put it mildly) path to travel down, and I ask her, in moments of unrelenting despair, "Where have you gone? Can you see me? Can you hear me? Can you give me a sign that you are somehow still with me?" And, then, thinking about the life WE had shared with one another and looking up at the stars in the night sky,

I feel that deep love WE had shared, a love that stretched to infinity and beyond. Our love was our light, and even in death, that light continues in my heart and soul. She is here with me now, even though she, just like those stars, has died.

***

This will be the closing chapter of this work. I have struggled as I have put my words and thoughts into print. At times, my grief has spilled out upon these pages. I have found myself crying and slipping into anxious moments, knowing full well what the reason for doing so is. It doesn't seem to matter that despite the many months that have flown by, I have not yet released (let go of) whatever it is that still clings to my mind and heart. I have not yet fully moved on, as loved ones encourage me to do. At times, I don't seem to be able to grasp where exactly I would move to or, for that matter, understand what "moving on" would entail. I know that I can interrupt my sadness by "getting out there," but I also know that interruptions are only temporary forms of solution. I have come to believe that grief is a much more complicated process than simply talking about the loss of the human being who willingly gave herself, her soul, to me, and I did the same to her. WE merged, and we now shine as one light in Indira's Net. Grief is, at this very moment, shaping the new person I am becoming today, tomorrow and the days beyond.

Gloria and I shared so many different interests while, at the same time, managing to maintain separate lives for ourselves. Separate lives, however, never meant, "I go this way, and you go that way." WE always sought the same destination and willingly shared different perceptions of how

243

to get there. WE both, like all couples, had moments when she went in one physical direction and I in another, but the depth of our love, loving each other more than WE loved ourselves, always kept us together, regardless of where WE were. WE always came home, and home was not simply a small or a large house: home was the connection between our souls.

***

It was an early December evening, and I was washing dishes following our supper. Gloria was stretched out on our living room couch, resting and watching those Christmas movies she so loved. With everything organized, I draped the dish towel on the oven door handle, wandered into the room and stood next to her, looking into her eyes. WE smiled at one another, and I reached down and took her hand in mine, pulling her carefully to her feet. "I have something I want to show you," I said as I began leading her through the kitchen, the den, and into my office. "What are you doing?" she inquired. "I want you to close your eyes and don't open them until I tell you to. Just follow me. I've got you." She did as I instructed and I led her to my office door, leading to our front yard, opened it, and carefully guided her into the chilly night air. Holding on to her, I said, "Now, open your eyes." As she did so she beheld before her our neighbor's front yard, which he had just finished decorating and lighting for Christmas. It was absolutely beautiful. There was a manger scene and a sleigh with Santa and his reindeer getting ready to go to work, fully lit for those passing by to see. There was an Angel surrounded in white, shining light, situated on the top of his house. And the house itself and the trees and shrubbery in his yard were strung with Christmas lights of every color imaginable.

"Oh my God," she softly uttered, and she quietly began to cry. WE held on to each other, just loving, and I then gently guided her back into the house as I explained to her that there was one more request for her time on my part. Again, I asked her to follow me as I led her into our kitchen. Stopping next to our counter, her hand still in mine, I instructed Alexa to play Jeff Healey's Angel Eyes. I pulled her close to me, draped my arms around her, and slowly, carefully, began to move my feet in a slow waltz. She followed my movements, leaning into my body. That was to be our last dance together. It seems as though an eternity has flown by since Gloria slipped away to places I am unable to see or comprehend. She is gone. And yet, I sense that even in her physical absence, she is, in some inexplicable way, here with me, perhaps even more than she ever was before her death.

I believe that if you, the reader, have managed to stay with my memories, my thoughts, and my ramblings for this long, you may also have a need to heal or, perhaps, to help others to heal. I hope that our story of love and loss may offer you some assistance in that direction. As we journey through our lives, we become aware of the fact that we will be wounded: wounds are a part of life. Some wounds may be so severe, so impactful upon our being, that we will not survive them. Other wounds may alter our chosen direction, but we will survive and go on. The wound of losing that which we love more than we love ourselves places us squarely at the crossroads of life. In losing, we oftentimes find ourselves alone, without a compass to guide us through what is next to come. I have experienced such a wound. I have struggled with the confusion of not knowing in which direction I should go. But choose I must, and so must you. So. I thank you for spending time with me as I have talked about my journey.

***

Luke and I awake. I brush my teeth, dress, and head into the kitchen to make my one cup of coffee for the day (I like more cream than coffee). It is overcast this morning, but the temperature is in the mid-seventies, and there is no wind. With a cup in hand, I open the door to the back porch and we both head outside. Luke goes immediately into the backyard to pee and "sniff," looking for whatever of interest he can find. I survey the plants, which are still beautiful and full of color, and I seat myself in a chair facing the bird feeders.

After completing his business, Luke joins me, lying close by my feet, quietly surveying the backyard, awaiting his next adventure. Gloria is with us, but I can't see her with my eyes; I just know. I feel calm and at peace, and I wonder how long that will last. I know that, at least for this moment in time, all is right with the world….

Four months after Gloria's death, I finished writing what I call GLORIA's SONG. Two months later, I carried my guitar into my first grief group meeting and through my tears and anxiety, I sang to them the following words:

GLORIA'S SONG

When we first met
And your eyes touched mine
We took an oath
To the end of time
Then we joined hands
And said I do
And I spent my life Loving you
As the years went passing by
You taught me how to live
You taught me how to love
And you taught me how to give
As the years went passing by
You taught me how to cry
And then one night
You taught me how to die

Now soar above this world you love
Let your spirit fill the sky
Paint the dark night with your bright light
Know we'll never say goodbye
Yes, I know you had to leave me
I know you couldn't stay
You closed your eyes, spread your wings
And then you flew away
Now my days have been so lonely
And my nights have been so long
Seems the pain, it never leaves me

It brings me to my knees
Memories replace my sight
You've gone to places I can't see
And I hear a voice from high above
Say, this is our destiny
Now soar above this world you love
Let your spirit fill the sky
Paint the dark night, with your bright light
Know we'll never say goodbye
Yes, I know you could not linger
I know you could not stay
Yes, I know you had to leave me
Then you turned and flew away
It was so easy loving you
I still want you here with me
But I know that you're not hurting
The Lord has set you free

I LOVE YOU UNCHINGO

Tomas-11/24